Treasured

Loving Elizabeth Book 3

A Pride and Prejudice Novella

Rose Fairbanks

Treasured

Published by Rose Fairbanks

ISBN: 9781790538423

Early drafts of this work were posted online.

Several passages in this novel are paraphrased from the works of Jane Austen.

Table of Contents

Also by Rose Fairbanks

Jane Austen Re-Imaginings Series
(Stand Alone Series)
Letters from the Heart
Undone Business
No Cause to Repine
Love Lasts Longest
Mr. Darcy's Kindness
Mr. Darcy's Compassion (Coming 2019)

When Love Blooms Series
Sufficient Encouragement
Renewed Hope
Extraordinary Devotion

Loving Elizabeth Series
Pledged
Reunited
Treasured

Pride and Prejudice and Bluestockings
Mr. Darcy's Bluestocking Bride
Lady Darcy's Bluestocking Club (Coming 2019)

Impertinent Daughters Series

The Gentleman's Impertinent Daughter

Mr. Darcy's Impertinent Daughter (Coming 2019)

Desire and Obligation Series

A Sense of Obligation

Domestic Felicity (Coming 2019)

Christmas with Jane

Once Upon a December

Mr. Darcy's Miracle at Longbourn

How Darcy Saved Christmas

Men of Austen

The Secrets of Pemberley

The Secrets of Donwell Abbey (Emma Variation, Coming 2019)

Regency Romance

Flowers of Scotland (Marriage Maker Series)

The Maid of Inverness

Paranormal Regency Fairy Tale

Cinderella's Phantom Prince and Beauty's Mirror (with Jenni James)

Dedication

To Ginna, she never stopped reminding me that "The Bennet Brother" needed to be finished. Her patience was rewarded. After five years, she got 3 books instead of one!

Chapter One

November 1, 1811

Three weeks after Reunited ends

Will arrived at Netherfield's stables and tossed the reins of Apollo at the ready hands of a boy. Charles arrived just after him—he had lost another race. Both gentlemen had smiles on their faces from their visit at Longbourn, but Will had an extra bounce in his step that made him feel lighter than air as he walked to the house.

The last few weeks of his engagement to Elizabeth had never ceased to amaze him. He could not be bitter about the past and their separation if it created the sweetness they shared since their reunion. Their estrangement made Elizabeth dearer to him now than she ever could have been without the years of misery. Now, after years of waiting, they were just over three weeks from their wedding day. Will's heart could scarcely contain its joy.

"Ah, Mr. Darcy," the butler said upon Will's entry. "The mail has just arrived. These are for you." He extended a handful of letters.

Taking the offered pile, Will thanked the man and sequestered himself in the library. Georgiana and Mrs. Annesley would be arriving any day, escorted by Richard. Several of his Fitzwilliam relations hoped to come for the wedding, as well. Lady Catherine had not been invited after Will learned she had schemed with her parson to end his engagement.

Apparently, Will's father had written to Lady Catherine about Will's attachment to Elizabeth years ago. When Lady Catherine learned of her parson's relationship to the Bennets of Longbourn and also learned of Will travelling to the area, she put two and two together. Mr. Collins needed a wife; all the better if it were one who would inherit Longbourn as the entail was broken. However, once she perceived Elizabeth Bennet as a threat once more, she commanded Collins to marry her—compromise her if he must.

Will's letters contained the usual news from his steward and housekeepers. Mrs. Annesley reported that Georgiana continued to be alternately withdrawn and angry. Richard confirmed he would escort the ladies. Lady Catherine spewed vitriol on the page. Her daughter wrote begging not to be painted with the same brush as her mother.

Weeks ago, when Elizabeth had first suggested that Will seek out proof from the post offices which might have been the source of the interference in his letters to her, he wrote to each of them. He had heard from most of them by now. Every office confirmed what the very first one had indicated. Wickham paid an employee to hand over Will's letters to Elizabeth. Why Wickham had wanted to disrupt those letters, Will had not yet determined.

He had also suspected Wickham of sabotaging his carriage. To find him, Will hired Bow Street Runners and had Richard ask around Wickham's favourite haunts in London. Wickham had been in Lincolnshire during the time in question. It appeared the incident with the carriage was a genuine accident.

Now, Will held in his hand a letter from the last post office in Scotland. They had never journeyed further north than this office, for the fire put an end to all those plans. Even now, Will could smell the stench of burning fabric and flesh, the thick smoke that had clogged his lungs and caused his eyes to burn. Merely reading the name of the town brought him back to that awful night.

Someone knocked on the door and, to distract himself, Will called for the person to enter. Charles greeted Will and settled in a chair near him.

"Another letter from a post office?"

"How did you know?"

"You have a certain look about you when they arrive. Is this the one, then?"

"And how did you know that?" Will was unused to Charles being so observant.

"For starters, I believe all the others are accounted for. Secondly, it's the only one that you would avoid and put off, and I see that the seal is unopened. Lastly, your expression was the same as it always is when the fire is mentioned." He paused and watched his friend. "Yes, that is the look exactly!"

Although Will did not have a looking glass to see what Charles referenced, he could feel the tightness of his muscles and the way his jaw clenched. It felt like turning to stone. "Very well," Will admitted. "It is the last dreaded reply. I do not know why I bother reading them. They all say the same thing, and there is nothing much I can do about it."

"You have always believed there was strength in knowledge. One day, you will meet Wickham again and will have your means to prove his deeds." Charles hesitated. While looking out a window, rather than meeting Will's eyes, he suggested, "Would you prefer me to read it?"

For a moment, Will was offended at the suggestion. Did Charles believe Will insufficiently strong to live with the reminder of the worst night of his life? Then, he considered how Elizabeth would react to the news. She was showing him what it meant to have unfailing support in his life. Charles had always attempted to be there, but Will would often push him out. He was working hard to overcome this flaw. It had caused enough heartache.

"I appreciate the offer," Will answered, at last, "but I believe I can read it. Knowledge of its likely contents makes it easier."

Swelling his courage, Will turned the paper over and tore open the seal.

Dear Mr. Darcy,

I could hardly contain my surprise at seeing a letter from you after all these years. You, undoubtedly, do not recall me, but I remember you and your traveling companions most vividly. However, I had expected a message from you many years ago.

You may ask how I can remember you so well. It is not often that our town loses its inn and its post office in one night.

Will furrowed his brows. He had forgotten; in this particular town, the post office was a mere corner of the inn.

Even more so when it is a victim of arson.

Will's grip on the paper tightened, and Charles glanced at him in concern at the crinkling noise. He could not answer his friend's unspoken question. He had to read on.

As such, all letters would have been lost. During the investigation into the fire, we discovered an employee had been bribed into taking several letters of yours and giving them to a gentleman who he believed to be traveling with you. The employee has been cleared of starting the fire, and unfortunately, the culprit is still at large. Oil and tar were used in the fire and buckets of each were found in one of the stables. No other clues had been discovered. No motive was ever established.

The incident is still much talked about, as the owner and a few others outside of your party perished. Eyewitness accounts have become a local legend and will soon fade into complete myth. It seems many believe the Greek god of fire is a lanky fellow with sandy blonde hair.

I had expected you to be more curious about the nature of the fire or the fate of your letters, but I suppose the losses you sustained that evening and the subsequent burdens you faced were of primary concern.

I regret that I did not have pleasanter news.

All my respect,

C. Whitaker

Will's mouth went dry as he read and reread the words. His father and Sam died in an arson? Who would have cause to start the blaze? Although Will had not known any of the other guests, he supposed only one would have such a strong motive. George Darcy had just settled his will, and Wickham knew he would be amply rewarded in it. Although he had ultimately rejected the living at Kympton, he asked for a handsome sum in addition to the one thousand pound legacy left to him in Mr. Darcy's will.

Wickham—a murderer? He had killed his own godfather, a man he counted as friend and mentor. He had murdered Sam, who once had been like a brother to him. He had been the means of separating Will from Elizabeth, first by the letters and then from the effects of the fire. Dear God! Elizabeth!

The incident with the carriage—which so easily could have harmed or killed her—must have been his doing, even if he were out of town.

"Will!" Charles said as he attempted to pull the paper from Will's vice-like grip. "Let me see, man!"

Will let go of the paper and barely registered Charles' tones of shock and violent anger. He too had considered it must have been Wickham.

"I never thought to ask about the source of the fire," Charles said. "It was too painful to think about. I wanted only to leave it in the past and forget about it as best I could."

Will silently nodded. "No investigators ever contacted me. No questions were ever asked." He could hear himself speak but felt removed from the scene.

"Do you see this? A lanky fellow with sandy hair. Could it have been Wickham?"

Again, Will nodded. This time, he was walking to the door when it happened. He was just about to call for his horse when Charles pulled him back into the room.

"What are you doing? Where are you going?"

"To find him!"

"You cannot do that on your own! Think!" Charles pushed Will into a seat and thrust a drink into his hand. "If he really did this—if he was behind the carriage in some way—he is too dangerous to approach. It may even be what he wants. You have always had what he desires, and he has proved he will stop at nothing to try and attain it."

Georgiana. Wickham's intended elopement now meant something entirely different. He not only wanted her fortune, but also her claim on Pemberley.

"Contact your cousin and the Runners again. Tell them to shadow Wickham closely. Report his every movement. Tell them everything!"

"Yes," Will said, his mind clearing with Charles' sound advice. "I shall hire guards as well. Until we have him in custody and are sure he does not have a proxy. A few here and some at Longbourn as well."

"I had not even considered Longbourn!" Colour drained from Charles' face. "However, if you have guards, then Wickham will perceive that we know of his plan."

Will noted Charles' reaction with shock. Was his friend thinking of Miss Bennet the way Will thought of Elizabeth? Now was not the time to worry about that but it would bear further consideration later. Unfortunately, he was correct about the guards. They did not wish to alert Wickham that they knew of his plot.

"Can I have my sister come? It may not be safe for her."

"She would be safer with you than away. He could more easily have access to her then."

"Indeed," Will said before swallowing the rest of his drink. Charles' words were far too true.

Will attempted to distract himself with other matters for the remainder of the day. All the while, he longed to return to Longbourn and sweep Elizabeth into his arms. He knew it was not true, but when he held her, he felt as though he could protect her from anything and battle any foe. As it was, his enemy was nigh on invisible.

Even if the Runners could be retained again and locate Wickham once more, it may not help. They had no real proof he had caused the fire all those years ago, and they had nothing but Will's gut pointing the destruction of his carriage axle to the man. Wickham had an alibi, and there was little use in trying to question him. He had someone else do his bidding, and while wondering how Wickham would have been able to afford to bribe someone, it was pointless to question how he came into the funds. He always did. He was worse than a cat with nine lives.

The possibility that everyone connected with Will would be a target ran through his mind without relent. If they could not find Wickham and make him confess, Elizabeth would never be safe. For that matter, if his end goal was Pemberley, neither was Georgiana. If the fiend had been willing to kill his godfather and friend, then there was nothing he would not do. Charles, Richard, the Bennets—none of them were safe, and all because they knew Will.

He pushed his chair from the desk and began pacing around the room. If he put everyone in danger, then he should leave. He should call for his horse now and return to London. His valet could bring the trunks tomorrow. Only...

Will had promised Elizabeth he would not leave again. Which was the greater risk? If he left, even with promises to return once all was resolved, it would break her heart. He had vowed to never be the source of her tears again. No catastrophe would draw him away otherwise. Should the worst happen at Pemberley, he would direct his steward and demand a hasty marriage from Mr. Bennet, or that she accompany him. He would not leave her behind again. However, if being near him put her at risk, then it would be selfish to remain.

Mentally exhausted and worried he would wear a hole in Charles' carpet, Will threw himself in a chair. Elizabeth's visage came to his mind as he considered how he would tell her of the development. She would cry, and each tear would sting like a dagger to his heart. Would she rant and rave? No, he thought not. She would not demand he stay when she believed his honour and affection for her should do the work for her. No, she would accept his words and a piece of her love for him would die.

He had already known what it was to lose her trust and how difficult it was to earn back. Could he do that again? Could he intentionally put them through that pain once more to apprehend Wickham?

Could he risk losing her affection and love forever, any hope of a future—to keep her alive? It would be a hollow victory indeed for Elizabeth to live but never marry him.

Will had sent an express to Richard as soon as he finished speaking with Charles earlier in the day. Before he went to bed that night, Will received a reply from his cousin. Richard was leaving that very instant—as soon his missive finished—to journey to Pemberley early and escort Mrs. Annesley and Georgiana to London. He agreed that having Georgiana near Will presented a problem. However, so did leaving her unattended, and Richard could not forsake his duties for long. Richard contacted the Runners once more and set about inquiries for footmen. He also asked if they should tell the earl.

Will as of two minds on the matter. The earl had been a very great friend to his father and had never been too intrusive in Will's own affairs once he became master. Lord Fitzwilliam was aging, and most of his duties were now executed by his eldest son, the viscount. Will had no quarrel with his older cousin. However, he desired to limit something so personal as his ongoing dispute with Wickham to as few people as possible. The rest of the Fitzwilliam family did not know about Georgiana's attempted elopement with Wickham. Even Richard did not know about her continued affection for the scoundrel.

When uncertain on who to trust, Will had always kept to his own counsel. He had thought in the future Elizabeth would support him through such times. Now, there was every possibility that there was no future for them. He could not ask her to wait on him once more.

Chapter Two

Elizabeth smiled as she rose for the day and went through her morning ablutions. Since the incident with Collins several weeks ago, she and Will had never been closer. The time of their wedding was rapidly approaching, and soon his family would arrive.

Will had been circumspect regarding his sister. He had told Elizabeth about Georgiana's intended elopement and that she continued to hold Wickham in high regard. What they had barely discussed was how Will felt about it all, and how his relationship with his sister stood. From what Elizabeth gathered, however, it was very strained. Just after the incident, Georgiana spent time at Pemberley, and Will stayed in London. Then, he came to Hertfordshire. It seemed there had been no time for the two to mend broken bridges and address old hurts.

It was hardly surprising. After all, there were more than ten years between the two. There had been only seven years between Elizabeth and Sam, but he would not reveal much to her, either. In the same way, Elizabeth was no more open to her youngest sisters. For example, she did not spend much time with Mary, despite the mere three years between them, as she was so new to society.

Tying her hair up with cheerful ribbons, Elizabeth pushed worries about Georgiana's arrival aside. Will would be calling soon, and the weather looked very fine. She hoped they would have some time to walk in privacy. In the weeks of their courtship, there was much they discussed which had never been canvassed before. Excitement filled her heart at the idea of learning more and more about Will Darcy for the rest of her life.

Elizabeth entered the breakfast room and greeted her family. Upon sitting, she and Jane immediately began whispering about possible contrivances for solitude with their suitors.

Mary peered at them from across the table. "I hope you are not expecting me to chaperone you forever." She slathered jam on her toast.

"Forever?" Elizabeth laughed. "Certainly not! I will soon wed." She looked at Jane with dancing eyes. "It is Jane who will need the chaperone."

"I thank you not to tease your sister, Miss Lizzy," Mrs. Bennet said. "You may work the fastest at ensnaring a husband, but we will see if he can come to the point at last. Mark my words, Jane has a far better chance of catching Mr. Bingley than you do of getting Mr. Darcy to the altar."

Elizabeth repressed the urge to roll her eyes. Her mother and Charlotte had not relented in their opinion that Will should not be trusted and would find some way to throw her over before the wedding. How they thought that would be possible when the settlement had been signed, in addition to the engagement being announced and well known in the neighborhood, she did not know.

As often was the case with her step-mother's anxieties, Elizabeth pretended they did not exist. There was no use in arguing about it. Mrs. Bennet no longer barred Will from entry into the house, and once they were married, her argument would have no legs to stand on. As it was, she did everything a mother should when their daughter was engaged. Despite Mrs. Bennet's rejection of her future son, Elizabeth did not feel slighted in the least.

"This afternoon, after the gentlemen have called, we must go into Meryton and begin shopping for your wedding clothes. Jane and Mary shall accompany us."

"Mama," Mary whined. "I will come, but only because I desired to stop at the bookstore as well."

"Of course, you may select a new book, my dear," Mrs. Bennet answered. "However, you will join us at the dressmakers and the milliner. It is good for you to be seen with your betrothed sister and for you to witness the goings-on before a lady marries. Your sisters accompanied Charlotte Lucas when she was selecting her things for Sam."

For a moment, no one spoke. Elizabeth had shared with Jane the truth about Sam's behaviour towards Charlotte. No one had told Mary. However, she was deeply reflective, and so Elizabeth would not be surprised to hear that the girl suspected much of the truth.

The rest of breakfast passed in the usual way. Then, Mrs. Bennet went upstairs to see to Kitty and Lydia's lessons. Mary took to the pianoforte, which left Jane and Elizabeth to each other.

"Mr. Bingley has been calling at Longhorn nearly as much as Will," Elizabeth said while sneaking a slight glance at Jane. "I wonder why?"

"Lizzy, do not tease me so." Jane blushed, but she smiled. "You must know my hopes by now."

"How can I know them when you have never said them?" Elizabeth batted her eyes at her elder sister, hoping she would fully and openly state her feelings.

"I never met such a man...that is, no one else has seemed..." Jane trailed off before gripping her hands and shaking her head. "Oh, how do you do this so much?"

"Do what?"

"Speak of your feelings so freely!"

Elizabeth straightened in her seat. She had not thought that she spoke so freely of her feelings. It is not as though she told anybody but Jane that she loved Will. She informed Mr. Collins that she was engaged to Will only as the most desperate measure.

Jane looked at her. "I do not mean only about Will. You speak freely about any number of things."

Elizabeth nodded in understanding. "I suppose it is that I have a very irreverent attitude towards the world in general. I do not care what they think of me very much." Troubled lines threatened to mar her countenance and Elizabeth struggled to keep her face neutral. The fact was, she worried very much that her attitude would not be welcomed in London society as Mrs. Darcy.

"It is not as though I fear what people will think. I simply hate for them to know."

"Dearest Jane, that is not a wrong sentiment. You are reserved, and I am not."

"I wish I could be more open," Jane said while staring at her hands. "I sense Mr. Bingley waits for some sign from me. It is as though he is dependent upon me declaring myself. I question how to reassure him of my interest."

"Perhaps all you need is time." Elizabeth laughed. "I know I should hardly be the one giving such advice, given the nature of my romance. However, it may be that Mr. Bingley needs time to know his own feelings and to be sure that he sees yours. Trust me, words come very easily to some and actions are much harder to prove."

"That is quite correct," Jane agreed. "Here they come now." She nodded to the window as they heard horses arrive on the drive.

Will and Charles were announced into the room, and Mary came to sit with them. After the usual pleasantries, Charles asked if they could go on a walk.

Mary let out a long-suffering sigh. "If you will wait in the hall and allow me time to gather a book I would be most happy."

Elizabeth gave her sister a guilty smile. She could hardly suppose Mary very much enjoyed chaperoning her older sisters. It disrupted her usual routine, and with two couples she was nearly always excluded. At least when Elizabeth would chaperone Charlotte and her brother, Jane would go with her.

At first, the five young people walked together. Soon, Will whispered to Elizabeth. He needed to speak with her in private. Elizabeth signaled to Jane, and their previously thought out plan was put into place. Mary had brought a book with her and did not seem to care or notice that her charges were dividing up in addition to putting considerable distance between her and them.

Will slowed his walk and nodded to a copse of trees next to the path. Elizabeth grinned in response and soon Will lead them to the privacy of the forest.

Elizabeth could feel, however, that something weighed on Will's mind. He had not appeared at ease when he had spoken earlier. More than this, he held her hand tighter than usual and pulled them to greater isolation than he usually would.

"Will," Elizabeth said as she tugged on his hand.

Will looked back at her, taking in her flushed cheeks and how she panted from the exertion. He suddenly stopped and pulled Elizabeth into his arms in a crushing embrace.

Elizabeth said nothing. She merely allowed Will to draw the comfort he so obviously needed from her. He tugged on her bonnet strings. In the last several weeks, had become more adept at untying them. Elizabeth removed the hat from her head, and it tumbled from her hands when he captured her lips.

The kiss was not as passionate or crazed as she had expected from his demeanour. However, there appeared to be a sense of desperation about him. He tenderly kissed every inch of her face and seemed to memorize the shape and feel of her lips before letting go and resting his head atop hers.

"I love you," Elizabeth sighed, and Will's arms tightened around her further. She pulled back to look at him, for he said nothing return. She heard a crinkling sound from his pocket.

"Tell me what worries you," Elizabeth said, and pushed a stray lock out of Will's eye. For a fleeting moment, it looked as though her movement brought Will pain. She pulled her hand back in concern and confusion.

"I cannot do it, Lizzy. I cannot. Not again." He squeezed her tightly once more.

Elizabeth hardly knew what think. He had never called her Lizzy before, but now was not the correct time to worry about it. "I would counsel you, if that is what you desire. However, I do not know what concerns afflict you."

Will remained mute, but his expression spoke for him. Everything about him appeared more rigid and austere. She recognized it as the same expression he wore when his father had reminded him of his duty all those years ago. He was afraid of something; he was scared of failing. He was torn and conflicted. She hardly knew why, but felt her own anxiety rise in response to his. "Was it a letter? Is that what it is in your pocket?"

Will nodded and squeezed his eyes shut in what looked like resignation. Withdrawing the letter, he held it out to her. Elizabeth took it with trembling hands. What could it say that would upset him so? Dread filled her as she unfolded the paper. Whatever it was, it would likely affect them both.

Her eyes fell on the paper, as she greedily read every line. There were many which required multiple viewings. Her voice caught in her throat and tears welled in her eyes. "Do I do understand this correctly? Sam did not die in an accident? He was killed!"

"Yes," Will answered and his voice broke.

Elizabeth looked up to see tears in his eyes as well. "Your father, Mr. Bingley's father, and Sam.

They were...they were killed! Why? Who would do such a thing?"

Elizabeth crumpled in a heap on the ground. Will dropped to his knees and held her to his chest as she sobbed. Since Will's return, Elizabeth had not missed Sam as much. However, she had kept her grief for his death so firmly over the years, mere weeks could not reset it. Now, the pain came back with a vengeance.

Will said nothing as Elizabeth cried and took consolation. As she did, a part of her healed unexpectedly. This was what she had needed when she had first heard of Sam's death. She had longed for Will's embrace and expected his support. When they met again, she never thought she would have a chance to relive those feelings. However, that did not mean she was thankful he finally fulfilled the role of comforter if it came at this cost.

Beginning to calm, she thought over the letter once more. Will's reaction was different from hers. It was not a concern of reliving the anguish of losing his father and friend that brought him pain. Unable to discern his feelings, Elizabeth turned her mind to other matters.

The post office clerk mentioned witnesses had seen a man with sandy blonde hair. Could it have been Wickham? He had traveled with them, and they already knew that he took Will's letters. They could discern no motive for him to steal the mail. However, Elizabeth could not understand why he would want to kill Mr. Darcy.

In the weeks since the incident, Elizabeth had not forgotten about the carriage axle which broke on her way to Netherfield. Someone had designed to kill Will. Was this related? If so, why wait so long before attempting to murder the son?

Elizabeth drew back and met Will's eyes, brushing away the tears that had fallen on his cheeks. "Do you have a suspect?"

Will's arms tightened around Elizabeth. "Wickham," Will said the word and a dark expression crossed face. "Who else? Who else is been such a bane to my very existence?"

"I am frightened," Elizabeth admitted. Throughout her life, she had relied on her courage. She could confess her fears only to Will.

"I am very sorry, love. I do not wish it..." His voice broke, and after a moment he attempted to speak again. "Perhaps it would be for the best..." He trailed off.

Chapter Three

Will kissed Elizabeth once more. After facing the truth of their loved ones' demise and all the emotion it brought on, their lips frantically met, drawing a different sort of comfort from one another. They were here, they were alive, they had this moment together.

Will tore his lips from hers and dropped his forehead to her shoulder. "How can I ask it of you? How can I bear it again?"

Suddenly, Elizabeth understood what Will had meant earlier. He was speaking of giving her up! Or at the very least, of postponing their marriage. Did she mean so little to him? Registering dampness on her gown, she realized Will cried at the thought of their separation. No, it was not that he desired this.

As though she had asked her question aloud, he spoke. "I would do anything to keep you safe, Elizabeth. Perhaps we are not meant to..."

Elizabeth pressed a finger to Will's lips to silence him. "Do not say it! We are meant to be together.

I have no intention of giving you up now or ever. You are mine, Will Darcy!"

She threw her arms around his neck. The unexpected movement knocked him to the ground. She leaned over Will and did not let go. In this position, they shared breath, and she could feel his heartbeat. Meeting his eyes, she considered her next words carefully. "I am not afraid at all for me. It is you that I worry about. It is you Wickham has targeted. If by some extreme misfortune, I am injured because I am with you or loved by you, I will gladly bear it. I would rather have one moment on this earth as your wife than live for one hundred years without you."

Will leaned up slightly and met her lips, then managed to reposition them so he had more dominance. After several minutes, Elizabeth pulled back, panting. "Love me, Will. Love me. Make me yours! No one can separate us once I am yours."

Will groaned and rolled away from Elizabeth. The distance returned Elizabeth's senses to her. What had she done? She had just thrown herself at Will and begged for him to defile her in the woods. She was worse than some common harlot!

Shame slapped her cheeks, but curiosity made her glace at her betrothed. He did not appear angry or displeased.

"Forgive me," Elizabeth reached forward and touched Will's arm.

His body jumped in response. "Leave me be, Elizabeth. Do not touch me just now."

The last time he had spoken so coldly to her was after Apollo had nearly trampled them and she asked after the scarred flesh on his arm. She had demurred then but would not this time. She made her choice not the least because if Will deserved her anger, she had no room for feeling ashamed of her behaviour.

"Do not shut me out," she said as she sat up. "You were willing to break our engagement—again! Are you still and that is why you do not desire my affections?"

Will rolled to face her and propped his head up with a bent arm. "I desire your touch and affection far too much. What you asked for a moment ago has been in my mind nearly unceasingly since shortly after I met you. I will not take your virtue until our wedding night. I am not the rake you thought I was."

Elizabeth huffed out a sigh and folded her arms tightly against her chest. "So we will have a wedding after all? Pray, sir, will it be before I am fifty? How shall I ever bear you a son at that age?"

"If it were legal at all, I would marry you this very minute. I would declare us wed with nothing but these trees as our witnesses. I do not want to break the engagement."

"May I know the stupid reason you had rationalized in your head that was worth giving me up? You were very incoherent just now."

Mischief lighted in Will's eyes. "I think you are proof at how eloquent I was."

His eyes raked over her, causing Elizabeth to realise the damage to her gown and hair. She blushed and glanced around for hairpins. However, she would not let him avoid the point. Rolling her hair up, she glared at him. "You know of what I speak!"

"You know what thoughts were in my mind, for you already argued against them. You were in the carriage! I cannot be so selfish!"

Elizabeth reached for Will's hand, and this time he did not shake her off. "There are times when I can perceive your thoughts or emotions and times when I cannot. Either way, I think it is best for us to talk about them openly and to each other. We should not presume to know the other's mind on such matters. It has only brought heartache too many times."

Will stood and reached for Elizabeth's hands, assisting her to her feet. "You are correct, Elizabeth. I will try to remember in the future. Can you forgive me?"

Elizabeth smirked as she tied the ribbons to her bonnet and dusted off her gown. "Only if you continue to kiss me like that and call me Lizzy."

Desire flashed in Will's eyes, and Elizabeth fought back a giggle. She had asked for him to be more open and he seemed quite willing to comply.

"Careful, minx," he said. "Too much temptation might send me to an early grave, and you seem to want me to survive for many years."

"For that, your penance will be—"

Will interrupted her saucy reply with more delicious kisses before tucking her hand on his arm. "We must return now, Lizzy," he whispered in her ear before directing her to the path.

They found Mary on a stump with her book. Jane and Charles were returning from further ahead on the path, and both wore enormous smiles. Mary raised her brows at each of them but held her chastisement. In the world of sisters, secrets were closely guarded, and Elizabeth felt she would have some recompense to pay for Mary's silence.

Will and Charles sat with the Bennets for another quarter of an hour after returning to the house. However, Will was hoping to hear from Richard and needed to be at Netherfield. Soon after they arrived, he heard a noise on the gravel drive. It was not the sound of a lone express rider as he had expected. Instead, Will heard the unmistakable sound of a chaise and four. Although curious, he had determined it could not be for him and continued to focus on the work at hand. The butler disturbing his solitude in the library with the announcement of his cousin, sister, and her companion exceedingly shocked him.

"Richard! Georgiana!" Will said as he glanced between the two. "I did not expect you for several days."

"Indeed," Richard said as he helped himself to Charles' port. "Soon after I wrote to you, I also sent a note to your housekeeper in town and informed her of when we would arrive. Imagine my surprise when she replied stating Georgiana had just arrived from Pemberley."

"I see," Will said as he considered Richard's information. Mrs. Annesley would have requested to change the plans. Only Georgiana's stubborn insistence would lead to the older woman disregarding his orders. However, it was unusual that she did not send a message as the journey from Pemberley to London took three days.

"You did not receive my express?" Mrs. Annesley asked.

"No. I am afraid not."

"How curious!" Georgiana said and pulled Will's eyes to her.

Indeed. How curious that yet another letter to him did not arrive. "And why were you in London?"

"Miss Bingley wrote that she was bored at Netherfield and expected to soon be in town. I had messages from many friends that they were already there."

"Did you?" Will met Mrs. Annesley's eyes. In his correspondence with her, she had expressed concern that her charge was receiving more letters than she considered regular, and that Georgiana was very evasive in answering questions about them. She guarded her privacy about the letters. "I fail to see how, simply because others were in one area, it meant you also needed to be present."

"Come, you cannot refuse me entrance to my own home."

Will raised his brows. "I suppose that means if they were all in Bath or elsewhere you would not choose to go there?"

"The countryside is so dull," Georgiana played with lint on her gown. "Although, I did come here as bidden like a good little girl." She made a face at her final words as though she had sucked on a lemon.

"Regardless of your feelings about where you are set to reside, you should remember that you are not of age to make such decisions, nor do you have access to your funds. You broke my trust at Ramsgate and again by leaving Pemberley—"

"No one has said that I left. You blame me for everything!"

"No, my dear," Will said sternly. "It is that I know Mrs. Annesley would not leave so recklessly."

"You trust a servant more than your sister!"

"Yes, I do!" Will stood and walked to his sister. "She has shown herself to have more honour than you at this moment."

"Will," Charles' red hair emerged in the doorway. "Wilson said that—" He entered and caught sight of the ladies. "Miss Darcy! You are here!"

"Charles," Richard raised his glass to his host.

"And Richard, too! Well, now I truly feel like a host! Good day to you all," he bowed to the room. "Welcome! If you are comfortable here for now, then I will alert the housekeeper, and we shall have rooms readied for you. Miss Darcy, I know my sisters will enjoy your visit and—"

"Thank you, Charles," Will interrupted. "Georgiana was just saying how tired she is and so I know she will appreciate a room as quickly as possible."

"Indeed!" Charles glanced between Will and the others and seemed to suddenly perceive the tension that had gone unnoticed before. "I will see to it immediately."

After he left the room and the door was shut, assuring some privacy, Will turned to his sister again.

Georgiana met Will's eyes with a mocking expression. Where was the sweet girl he once knew? Where had he gone wrong with her? What choice in his past did he make which led to this? Sighing, he decided to tell her the truth. "Georgiana, I have not asked you here to ruin any plans of yours. If you had desired to come to London, then I could have responsibly arranged such things. As it happens, I believe you must have insisted you would go without an escort, but we will address that later. First, I desired you here so you might become reacquainted with your future sister-in-law."

Georgiana gasped, "Sister-in-law! I had thought you never meant to marry."

"It is true, for years I thought I never would. But I have become reacquainted with the lady that I have admired since our first meeting five years ago."

"Who do you mean? Not Miss Bingley!"

"I should say not! Miss Elizabeth Bennet of Longbourn has accepted my proposal, and we are to wed in three weeks' time."

Will watched in consternation as Georgiana's expression changed from repugnance to shock to something entirely unreadable. It was not the reaction had expected from his sister. "I believe you quite enjoyed your time with her while she stayed at Darcy house."

"Enjoy would be a stretch. I was a child confined to the nursery. Papa only brought me down to impress his friends. Nor could I control who came and went in my room. Yes, the Miss Bennets frequented the nursery, but do not imagine we became friends." Georgiana raised her chin in defiance.

Will furrowed his brows and looked at Mrs. Annesley then Richard for clues as to why Georgiana would react this way. Their expressions seemed as clueless as his. "I am sorry to hear that, but I know you will not allow experiences from so long ago to cloud your vision."

"Like they did for you? Once a fortune hunter always a fortune hunter."

Georgiana sniffed, and her expression was far too much like Caroline Bingley for Will's taste. "That is enough," he said but did not raise his voice. Then, glaring at his sister, he continued, "Elizabeth Bennet was never a fortune hunter, and I have never mentioned that fear to you. I can think of only one who could have, and I wonder why he would. Georgiana, ask yourself why your friend Wickham would need to slander the name of a guest in your father's house and a lady of whom your brother thought well."

Georgiana looked at her nails distractedly. "I am sure he told me so I could see how your judgment is not always perfect. The blinders are off now, dear brother. You may order me about, as you legally can. However, you will no longer influence my mind."

Anger clouded Will's vision. "Mrs. Annesley, Richard, I trust you will see my sister to her room when it is provided. I have said all that is necessary and now must return to my business. Georgiana," he looked at her. "If you can show yourself to be civil at dinner, you may accompany the Miss Bennets and Miss Bingley to the shops in Meryton on Monday." Will stiffly bowed and had just reached the door when Richard called after him.

"Have you not forgotten to tell her of a rather critical development?"

"Ah, yes." Will glanced over his shoulder at his sister. "You should perhaps be forewarned that we have every reason to believe that the man who hoped to seduce you has also murdered our father, as well as Mr. Bingley's father, and Miss Elizabeth's brother. The fire was arson and witnesses describe a man like Wickham. There have been strange and dangerous incidents since I have been at Netherfield, targeting myself and Miss Elizabeth. Besides my desire for you to reacquaint yourself with my betrothed, there is a genuine fear that Wickham might try to harm you, or contact you in some way."

Will examined his sister for a long moment. "Has he?"

"No," she answered.

Will found he could not believe her words.

“Surely what you say is impossible. Wickham would never be—”

“He would. He would, indeed.” Will turned and left for his chamber.

Chapter Four

On Monday morning, Elizabeth, Jane, and Mary awaited Georgiana's arrival at Longbourn. When, at last, the carriage arrived, no one got out.

After waiting several minutes, Jane broke the silence. "Perhaps she does not wish to leave the coach."

"This is most unusual," Elizabeth said. "For I know Will desired her to come in and meet the family."

"I can hardly blame her for not wanting to meet any of us," Mary interjected. "What are we to the Darcys? We should go to her."

"I suppose so," said Elizabeth. "Although, Will had wanted her to come and greet the family."

"I daresay if your Will truly wanted that to happen, he would have ridden with her," Mary observed.

Elizabeth forced herself not to reply to her sister's rather annoying opinion. "She was very shy as a young girl. Perhaps once we have shopped and chatted and gotten to know one other again, she shall be more willing to come inside."

"Yes, I think you are right, Lizzy," said Jane.

The girls collected their outerwear and walked to the coach. Once inside, conversation was nearly nonexistent. Thankfully, the journey to Meryton was a quick one. It was so short the girls often chose to walk. Elizabeth sighed to herself. This must be part of becoming Mrs. Darcy. She could not expect to have the freedom to walk to so many places any longer. As she observed Miss Darcy, it appeared to Elizabeth that an additional reason for the carriage was likely due to the younger girl's shopping habits. They would need the space for all of her purchases.

"Here we are," Elizabeth chirped.

"How quaint," Georgiana said in a disapproving tone.

"I am sure it is not as sophisticated as London," Mary said. "But it does have its charms."

"Indeed, Elizabeth said with a smile. "I recall from Sam's letters that the area around Pemberley was not as large and did not have as new styles. For a country town, I imagine Meryton might have more to offer in the way of shopping and people to meet than many others."

"I hope you will not miss it too much, Miss Elizabeth. You should know that my brother does not favor town, so on your marriage, you will be spending much time in the country, with far fewer shops and people to meet. I know many people are aghast when they learn my brother does not host lavish parties or run up bills at all the local shops."

Elizabeth glanced at Jane, confused at Georgiana's annoyed tone. "I assure you, Georgiana, I quite love the country and look forward to seeing my new home."

"I do wish for you to call me Miss Darcy. Additionally, you should know there is much more to running an estate as large as Pemberley than merely seeing all of its grand rooms and expensive furnishings."

"Indeed," Elizabeth said. "I did not mean to make it sound like anything else. I know Pemberley is larger than Longbourn, but I believe I am up to the task of managing it. Of course, with the help of you and the housekeeper." It was not worth the effort to be upset at the girl. If she could not hold her own against Will's sister, how would she ever manage London? The only way to deal with such ladies was by ignoring their attacks.

Georgiana laughed. "I am afraid I will of be no help. I shall spend most of my time in London. I take my lessons very seriously. Perhaps, I might teach you various accomplishments." Georgiana's eyes lingered on Mary and Jane. "If you ever invite your sisters, that is if Will ever believes they are worthy of my company, I should be happy to assist them as well."

Elizabeth was saved from having to reply further to Georgiana by the footman opening the door. One by one, he handed the ladies down. Once outside, Georgiana surveyed the square with a critical eye. If Elizabeth had thought Will was proud when they first met all those years ago, it was nothing compared to the expression of his sister.

"Where would you like to start, Miss Darcy?" asked Jane. "We have a milliner, a dressmaker, even a bookseller who sometimes gets music."

"Lizzy must go to the dressmaker and milliner, and Jane prefers those as well. However," said Mary, "if you would prefer the bookshop, I always come to visit it. I would welcome your opinion of our offerings compared to London's shops."

"What? Have you never been to town?

"No," Mary answered looking at her shoes. "I have just come out, and my relations have only ever invited Jane and Lizzy."

"You must not feel left out, Mary." Jane put her

arm around her sister. "You are out, and now that Lizzy is getting married there will be additional space in their home for you. Nor must you make it sound as though we were always visiting. There many years we could not as Aunt was too busy with the children."

"I know," Mary sighed.

"In that case," Georgiana said with a smile, "I do like your suggestion, Miss Mary."

"Really?" Mary asked in surprise.

"Indeed! Music is my greatest joy in life, and the instrument at Netherfield is quite nice. It does not compare to the one at Pemberley or even Darcy house, but it will do. However," Georgiana rolled her eyes, "I cannot abide by Miss Bingley's taste. I do not know that we shall find anything suitable here, but it is worth a look."

"I also greatly enjoy playing." Mary gave Georgiana a timid smile. "I am sure my talent is nothing to yours after training with Masters in town. If you desire to teach me, I very much would like to learn."

"Excellent!" Georgiana linked her arm through Mary's. "We should go to the bookshop and then meet your sisters at the dressmaker's." They began to step away.

Mary looked over her shoulder. "You do not mind, Lizzy, do you?

"Of course not," Elizabeth shook her head. "It is very appropriate for you to spend time together, especially as you have such similar interests. I also enjoy playing but lack the passion Mary has for it. I would love to hear you play again, Miss Darcy. I have very fond memories of it from years ago. You must be even more improved since then."

As Elizabeth and Jane made their way to the dressmaker and the milliner, Elizabeth could not help but wonder at Georgiana changing from the girl she had known five years ago. This Elizabeth could explain to herself. Georgiana was now at the most trying years of a young lady's life, and some alteration in mood and temperament would be expected. Her kindness to Mary would be proof that her ill-nature was not a permanent change, except that Elizabeth did not trust Georgiana was genuinely interested in Mary.

Mary was a year older, but Georgiana appeared the elder in many ways. Although she was the younger lady, Georgiana had gone to London and been in the world. She had already made the mistake of trusting George Wickham, and now believed brother tore her apart from a constant lover. Mary, by contrast, was quiet. The only common interests or experiences they could have would be the pianoforte. While Mary counted it as an accomplishment, she played mostly for enjoyment and did not have the skills at seventeen that Georgiana had at twelve. Georgiana had many years' worth of music masters. Mary did not usually separate from Jane and Elizabeth on their trips to Meryton, and it concerned Elizabeth how quickly Georgiana manipulated everyone around her.

Elizabeth's concerns seemed for naught, however, when Mary and Georgiana arrived at the dressmaker's in due time, none the worse for the wear. "How did you find the bookshop, Miss Darcy?" Elizabeth asked.

"Mary was quite correct. It is nothing compared to the sophisticated shops of London. However, it will do, and I did find this," she held up a package, "It is not as new as the pieces I find in town but far better than what Miss Bingley has at Netherfield."

"She bought me some pieces as well," Mary said with a blush.

"That was not necessary, Miss Darcy," Jane said. "We would have lent Mary the money if she did not have enough."

"Think nothing of it. There is nothing I would not do for my friend."

The expression Miss Darcy wore almost fooled Elizabeth. It likely would have convinced anyone else of her good intentions. Elizabeth wondered if Will knew how Georgiana spent her money. He was no spendthrift, and he would not approve of his sister becoming one. However, she did do something kind, and it was only music, so there was little reason to criticize.

"We wished to show you around the square, now," Jane said.

Elizabeth had expected Georgiana to refuse, but so few could ever decline anything Jane offered. Georgiana's lips turned up in a fake smile, and she linked her arm through Mary's. "I see no harm. Perhaps we will meet with some new acquaintances, as you seem so fond of doing, Miss Elizabeth."

Elizabeth thought she saw a look pass between Georgiana and Mary, but then decided it was merely due to her annoyance at Georgiana's behavior. They ambled along the square for some time before seeing Charlotte. Charlotte acknowledged them with a curtsy and a light blush. She looked as though she were on the verge of hastening away, but Jane called out her.

"Charlotte, how are you?" Jane asked.

"Tolerably well. I hope you and your family are in good health." She glanced at Elizabeth. "How do the wedding plans come?"

"We are all very well. Thank you for asking. Mama is making such a fuss about the wedding, but after having to wait for so long, I fear I quite like it."

Charlotte looked at Miss Darcy, and her eyes asked the unspoken question. Good manners dictated that Elizabeth must wait for Georgiana to request an introduction, but she doubted the girl would ask for one. The Bennet ladies continue to speak with Charlotte in stilted conversation, as Elizabeth and Charlotte had not entirely repaired their friendship.

At length, Charlotte turned to go and resume her activity when her eyes widened, and a new blush came to her cheeks. The others could not help glancing at whatever she had seen. The only thing Elizabeth could see of note was a young man in an officer's uniform, but he was not of the militia. He rode his mount quite well. He was no Fitzwilliam Darcy, and yet something about him reminded Elizabeth of her betrothed.

"Richard," Georgiana said surprised.

Elizabeth looked at the man with more interest as she now understood him to be Will's cousin.

She had met him years ago but did not recall his face. He directed his horse to their position.

"How do you do, Georgiana? Have you enjoyed your shopping?"

"I have found some music that meets my standards and the ladies are showing me around the square."

"Indeed, if I were a lady that sounds like an enjoyable morning. Would you introduce me to your new friends?"

"I will introduce who I can," Georgiana said.

One by one she introduced the Bennet sisters. After the usual civil replies, Georgiana looked expectantly at Elizabeth. The older girl sighed. She ought to have expected such behaviour from Will's sister, given her age and circumstances in life. Elizabeth had built fairy tales in her head about her future with Will, and they might never become a reality. Well, difficult sisters were not the worst of her worries. She drew her shoulders back.

"And this is our good friend Miss Charlotte Lucas." Elizabeth felt a twinge of remorse as the statement no longer felt true. "Her father is our local knight. You are certain to meet Sir William soon and see for yourself how very friendly he is."

"It is a pleasure to meet you, Miss Lucas," Colonel Fitzwilliam said with a twinkle in his eye men usually held only for Jane. His words seemed to have stirred Charlotte from a blushing stupor.

"For me as well," she said while directing her eyes past him.

"A friend to Miss Elizabeth is a friend to my cousin Will, and therefore a friend to me."

Charlotte frowned at the further mention of Will. "Likewise. Pardon me, I have forgotten that Mama needed me home by now."

Elizabeth watched as the woman who used to be her friend scurried away but peeked over her shoulder for one more look at them. How very curious.

"If you ladies are finished shopping, I will escort you to the carriage. I can follow Georgiana back from Longbourn and then she will not have to ride unchaperoned."

Georgiana looked displeased with the notion, but took her cousin's arm when he offered it. Between Elizabeth and Jane, they managed to chat with the Colonel until they reached the carriage. Georgiana remained resentfully silent, while Mary appeared more pensive.

Gallantly, the Colonel handed each lady in. When Elizabeth placed her hand in his, she felt an object slide into her fingers. Sneaking a peek at it once in the carriage, she saw a tightly folded piece of paper with a snippet of Will's handwriting. Her heart fluttered in her chest. How she loved notes from her betrothed. However, why did he not bring it to Longbourn? Or if he could not call, then he might have sought her out in Meryton, rather than sending his cousin.

The thoughts swirled in Elizabeth's head as the carriage began to pull away and its occupants were in discussion describing Longbourn to the Colonel. Elizabeth turned her head to view the passing scenery, and her heart nearly stuttered to a stop at what she saw. There, on the streets of Meryton, was George Wickham.

Chapter Five

Will tugged on his gloves in Netherfield's front hall. Charles ought to have arrived by now. After Richard decided to go for a ride through Meryton in hopes of finding Georgiana, Will determined his cousin and sister should not be the only ones seeing Elizabeth on this day. Speaking with Charles, they decided to ride to Longbourn. Finally, his friend arrived in the hall.

"You are looking more well-groomed than usual," Will said as he looked Charles over.

"It is an important day," Charles said and fiddled with his cufflinks.

"Is it?"

"You will pull it out of me, will you?"

Will playfully bumped into his friend's shoulder. "If it is important for the reason I think it is, then I should say if you find it so difficult to utter the words for me, then you will never survive your lady."

"My Bennet lady is far sweeter than yours," Charles said.

Will laughed as he recalled his several proposals to Elizabeth. She had been a bit demanding when he could barely string together a coherent thought. Jane surely would not put Charles through all that. "And her father?"

Charles ceased his movements. "He would not refuse would he?"

Will did not think Mr. Bennet would, but he would probably enjoy teasing his potential son-in-law. "I expect he will give no leniency if you beat around the matter. You are asking for his daughter's hand. He needs to see that you can be the man of the house."

Charles nodded and finally began walking toward the stables again. "I can be the man of the house. I am the man of the house!"

"Are you?" Will asked.

"As it happens," Charles said after mounting his horse, "Caroline and the Hursts will be returning to London shortly."

"This was your idea?"

"Yes," Charles nodded. "Not that I have explained it to them but if Wickham has intentions for you, they are safer in town. Secondly, I will not put up with Caroline and Louisa's mocking of Elizabeth or Jane. I have made my mind up and do not care for childish tantrums. If they do not like it here, they can go to London."

"And?"

Charles thought for a moment. "And I will inform Caroline she cannot go over her allowance. Extra time in town is not to be a reward for bad behavior."

"Excellent," Will said. Charles ought to have taken Caroline in hand years ago. However, as Will was discovering with Georgiana, it was not easy to restrain one's sister. He could only guess that their closeness in age created even more problems.

Will slapped the reins against his mount and raced off. "Catch up!" He grinned over his shoulder. "Or you will never beat me!"

"I did not know we were racing!" Charles called after him as he directed his horse to a gallop.

Arriving at Longbourn, Will immediately sensed something was wrong. The servant who answered the door looked at them warily and brought them to the drawing room where a pale Elizabeth sat drinking wine as Jane rubbed her back.

"Perhaps you were mistaken," Jane said.

“No. I know it was him,” Elizabeth replied.

Will cleared his throat, garnering Elizabeth’s notice. Before he had made more than two steps into the room, Elizabeth had raced to his arms and squeezed him tightly. “What is this? Are you well?”

“I am; are you?” Elizabeth pulled back and glanced over him.

Not understanding her behaviour, Will searched the room for Georgiana and Richard. They were not present. “Come, let us sit. You feel as cold as ice.”

Will led Elizabeth to a settee and rubbed her hands between his. “Miss Bennet, could you articulate for me what has scared Elizabeth nearly out of her wits?”

Jane looked at Mary before replying. “Elizabeth thinks she saw Mr. Wickham in Meryton.”

Instantly, Will’s body tensed. How could he be here? Did not Richard have Runners watching the scoundrel’s movements? He must have eluded them somehow. Where was Richard?

“Will!” Elizabeth cried.

Looking down, Will realised he was vigorously rubbing Elizabeth’s hands. He released them. “Forgive me.”

Taking a deep breath, he blew it out. She was safe, that much was clear. Additionally, Richard, wherever he was, had surely ensured Georgiana was safe. He had no reason for urgent action. Bingley had been correct earlier. The better route was to form a plan.

Fortunately, before Will had to ask about their whereabouts, Richard and Georgiana entered the drawing room. Richard's face was set in a stern and grim expression, while Georgiana visibly stiffened upon seeing Will. "I have been apprised of the situation. Did either of you see him? Georgiana, did he speak with you?"

"Of course, I did not speak with him," Georgiana said with flashing eyes that indicated annoyance. "I was never alone."

"Georgiana did separate from Miss Elizabeth and Miss Bennet," Richard supplied.

"I was getting better acquainted with Miss Mary," Georgiana interjected. She gave the lady a soft smile. "She did not leave my side, and I believe we shall become very good friends."

"Miss Mary, is this true?" Richard asked.

Will hated that he had to doubt his sister. He loathed that it was displayed for the Bennet ladies to see, and that his cousin had to take on the role as Will had already failed to protect Georgiana once.

"Yes," Mary nodded enthusiastically. "Miss Darcy and I went to the bookshop together. Jane and Lizzy had gone to the milliner."

"I did give them leave to go look at books without me," Elizabeth said. "I hope you are not angry with me."

Will shook his head and affectionately touched Elizabeth's hand. "I am not angry, my dear." He knew Georgiana well enough to suppose she had insisted on going. He would deal with that later. Now, the greater concern was Wickham. "Are you certain that it was he? You have not seen him in several years."

"I could not forget what he looks like. If I had greater sketching ability, I would draw his picture for you."

"Lizzy, might you be overwrought?" Jane asked. "You have been greatly concerned lately, and Mr. Wickham has featured prominently in those worries."

"I know what I saw!" Elizabeth turned to Will. "Do you believe me?"

“Yes, love. Richard and I shall discuss how we will discover why he is in this place and what his potential motives are.”

“Are we in danger?” Jane asked.

“Certainly not,” Charles said.

Will nearly jumped at the voice. He had forgotten his friend was here, as Charles had been uncharacteristically silent. “Charles is correct. We will do the best in our ability to protect you all, and he has nothing to gain from harming any of you. There is nothing to worry about.”

As Will said it, he forced himself to not cringe at the lie. The other girls probably had no reason to be concerned. Elizabeth, however, could be a target. Wickham would know that harming her would crush Will.

“Elizabeth, do you remember anything about where he was or what he wore? Were there any distinguishing features?” Will asked.”

Elizabeth thought in silence for a moment or two. “Now that I think about it, his coat looked like a militia uniform. I could not see most of his body, only his face.”

“And the location?”

“It was where our carriage was. Near the water pump.”

"There is a tavern nearby, and I suspect that is where we could find many other militiamen, if not the colonel of the regiment himself," Richard said.

"We will journey there ourselves as soon as we take Georgiana back to Netherfield."

"Must I go?" Georgiana turned to her brother and gave him a pleading look.

It had worked when she was a small child and wished for some trifling thing from him. Years ago, it had ceased to work, and she had used the tactic with less frequency. He distrusted her motives for attempting it now.

"You have visited long enough for one day."

"I thought I was invited to spend time with your betrothed?"

"And yet you did not," Will raised his brows. He would not publicly expose that she had arrived before the "invitation" was ever issued. However, he was not in a mood to indulge any of her requests. She had disobeyed him again.

"Allow me to rectify that now. Miss Elizabeth also enjoys music. We could play together." Georgiana sent Mary an apologetic look.

"That is a fine idea for your next meeting. It is useless to argue, though."

“Oh, I would not dream of arguing with you, dear brother.”

Georgiana stood and curtsied to her new friends, but it was done with an attitude Will did not like. If Elizabeth had less strength of character, he would wonder about bringing his sister around her, lest the poor behaviour rub off.

“Goodbye for now,” Georgiana said to the room while wearing a false smile. “I trust we shall meet again soon.”

Richard escorted her to the carriage while Will and Charles said farewell to their ladies. When Will grasped Elizabeth’s hand to bring it to his lips, he felt her tremble.

“Fear not, my love,” Will said. “We shall apprehend Wickham. You are in no danger. I will inform your father on my way out. This will soon be but yet another unpleasant memory.”

“It is not myself who I worry for but you. I have told you this,” Elizabeth whispered and glanced around anxiously. “Take care,” she squeezed his hands tightly, “for you carry my heart with you, and it could not survive another blow.”

Will had never ached to hold her more, but he could not gather her into his arms before her sisters. They had already broken propriety once while she was in the throes of distress. Soon, they would not have to separate, and she could always be with him. He placed a stray tendril behind her ear. "Everything shall be well," he promised.

While he had not felt the words when he said them earlier, he meant them now. Whatever it took to make Elizabeth happy again, to ease her worries and erase the concerned look in her eye and lines between her brow, he would do. A quick kiss to her hands, a short conversation with Mr. Bennet, and Will was climbing into the carriage within minutes.

Looking at his sister, he vowed, "It will not work."

"What will not work?" Georgiana asked and glanced nervously at Charles.

"I do not mind if he hears this," Will said. "I will explain all to him later. I reference your dear Wickham's scheme to have you ingratiate yourself with the Bennets."

"That is not what I was attempting to do!" Georgiana folded her arms over her chest.

"I could not care less if you liked them or they liked you. Elizabeth will be your sister, and you will have plenty of time to get to know her better once our marriage begins. I will not be bringing you with me on any subsequent calls at Longbourn until you earn my trust."

Georgiana said nothing. She glared angrily at Will for a moment before defiantly turning her head and staring out the window. Will nodded his head at her actions. She knew it was useless to argue. He would not budge on this.

They arrived at Netherfield after a silent and tense ride. Charles had wisely chosen not to speak. Miss Bingley met them in the drawing room.

"I would ask where you all wandered off to but with those scowls, I believe I can guess," she teased at the serious looks the men wore. "Mrs. Bennet's effusions always make me feel the same way. Colonel Fitzwilliam, do you not think it is absolutely intolerable that Mr. Darcy has aligned himself with such a woman?"

"We did not speak with Mrs. Bennet," Charles said before Richard could answer.

"You did not?" Caroline's brow furrowed. "Well, surely you did not speak to Mr. Bennet! I have never heard the man utter a word!"

"I did go to Longbourn with the intent of

speaking to Mr. Bennet about a courtship with his eldest daughter, who you call a friend," Charles hissed between grit teeth. "I have had enough of this, Caroline. Tell your maid to ready your trunks for tomorrow. I will inform Mr. Hurst as well."

"Surely you are not banishing me to London because of an ill-timed tease!"

"I am sending you to London so I may court the woman I love in peace. She deserves no less from me." He motioned to the door. "Now, go on your way. When I return, we will have a very candid conversation about your spending habits in town."

Caroline scurried off, calling out a mixture of disbelief at her treatment and vows to behave better, if only he did not cut her allowance. Charles murmured that he would speak with Hurst and then return.

Georgiana sulked to the door. "I suppose you will do the same to me," she said as she neared her brother.

"No. Go to your chamber, and we will speak to you when we return."

Georgiana nodded but hesitated for a moment. She looked back at Will with tears shimmering in her eyes. "I know it to be impossible for Wickham to behave as you have described. He would never hurt anyone and could never have hurt Father."

"Go now," Will said and shook his head. It was useless to try and convince her of anything just then.

While Richard and Will waited for Charles to finish speaking with his family, they came up with a general plan on how to approach Colonel Forster. When their friend returned, they apprised him of it before setting off for Meryton.

They came back two hours later with even more haggard expressions than they wore at their outset. George Wickham was a member of the militia and thus far an exemplary soldier. Will could hardly fathom the young man he knew happily doing such menial tasks. Other than a lifetime of taunting, spending his inheritance too quickly, and his attempting to seduce Will's sister, there was nothing to lay against the man—most of which Will would either not divulge or would not help his argument. In the end, they had no examples of Wickham's perfidy aside from his spending too freely. Colonel Forster sent them on their way with a promise to keep an eye on the man but would not have others picking on one of his officers, either.

As the evening wore on, Will wrote a message to Mr. Bennet informing him of the meeting, and ordered a tray to his room. He could not abide the theatrics of Charles' sisters or his own. One good thing came from Wickham's presence in the area; Caroline Bingley and her sister would be gone, and Will would have one less headache. As it was, he would need most of his concentration to affect confidence and security when calling at Longbourn, when in reality he felt nothing but sheer terror at the thought of Wickham hurting Elizabeth.

Chapter Six

The following morning, Elizabeth waited impatiently for Will to arrive. She did not know if he would bring Georgiana or not, but she rather doubted he would. Elizabeth did not know why Georgiana disliked her, but she also did not think it was worth much of her concern. While she waited, she spoke with Jane.

“Mr. Bingley was to ask Papa for permission to court me yesterday,” Jane said.

“And I ruined it!” Elizabeth shook her head. “Pray, forgive me. I did not intend to steal your happiness.”

“I know you did not mean to create a disturbance in our plans. Please, do not worry my behalf. I am only happy, no, happier that he will ask today. Now, the memory does not need to be marred with Wickham and your troubles.”

“Troubles, indeed.”

“Do you really think he is so evil? We did not know him for long. I do not think I even spoke to him. He seemed very gentlemanly, and Will's father enjoyed his company."

"You know what he tried to do to Miss Graves. Will tells me there were other ladies, too. If Wickham were willing to resort to such tactics with women, why would he stop there?"

"I suppose you are correct, but I hate thinking so."

"I know, dearest," Elizabeth embraced her sister. "You would rather go through all of life without realizing such evil existed. But it does. And unfortunately, it has seen fit to attach itself to Will."

"Lizzy," Jane began hesitantly. "Do you think... That is..." Jane sighed. "Well, is there not some sense in delaying the wedding? Why make yourself a potential target?"

"I have waited long enough to marry Will Darcy! I will not delay anything simply because of the tactics of George Wickham. I shall tell you what I told Will the other day on our walk. I would rather live one moment in this life as his wife than live one hundred years without him."

"No one is saying you ought to give him up for good. I only wonder if it should be postponed."

Elizabeth shook her head. “No. Too much as happened in our past. Too much has already been in the way. Could you imagine giving up Mr. Bingley?”

Jane sucked in a deep breath. “That would be very difficult.”

“Now imagine being asked to do it not once but twice, and all due to your own fear.” Elizabeth shrugged. “I will stand by him. He needs someone beside him.”

Jane sighed and looked out the window. “Then there is nothing left for me to say about the matter.”

“You are not any less stubborn than I am when you are convinced you are correct. You merely do it with more grace.

Jane smiled a little. “I do have more tact than you. However, I would not change you one bit.”

The conversation was interrupted by the entrance of Mary. She hummed a tune they had not heard before.

“What is that you are humming?” Elizabeth asked.

“Oh, you would not know it.” Mary shook her head and gave an exasperated sigh. “It is from Faniska and came out in Vienna a few years ago.

Miss Darcy tells me both Herr Beethoven and Herr Haydn applauded it." Mary sat down and pulled out some embroidery with a fond smile. "She bought the piece for me. It is the newest work I have ever had. You know how difficult it is to get the new pieces from the Continent, and they are so expensive."

"You seem to get along very well with her." Elizabeth watched her sister closely for signs that anything was irregular about her meeting with Miss Darcy. Additionally, it was peculiar that Mary was sitting with them at all, and desired to do something as mundane as needlework.

"I felt more akin to her than I do with nearly anyone else I have ever met in my life. I do hope we can become very great friends."

Elizabeth heart sunk a little for her sister. Jane and Elizabeth had never meant to exclude Mary, and yet they nearly always did. She was a few years younger than Elizabeth and the eldest of Fanny Bennet's daughters. Jane and Elizabeth had gone through things before Mary's birth which made them close. During those dark years, the sisters became inexplicably attached. The youngest sisters, Kitty and Lydia, were very close in age. They had similar temperaments, while Mary was more severe and yet was not included with the older girls. However, she was now out in society, and that should change the dynamics. Elizabeth, and most likely Jane, would soon marry, but that did not mean they could not speak with their sister in a more adult way. Marriage would not be too many years off for her, either. Before long, they would all be married ladies. Elizabeth mentally applauded herself for her rational thoughts. Yes, it did not matter if so far for the last seventeen years, they had not given Mary enough attention. They had far more than seventeen years ahead of their lives to make the difference.

"I hope Miss Darcy can visit today," Mary said as she pulled the needle through the fabric. "I do not like to say it, but I thought Mr. Darcy was a little harsh with his sister yesterday."

Jane touched Mary's arm. "He only appeared harsh to you because you have never had any critical words spoken to you. Miss Darcy needed correction, and her brother is her guardian. We have no business having any sort of opinion on the subject."

"You cannot tell me that you think everything he was saying and how he treated her was right."

There was an edge to Mary's voice Elizabeth had not heard before. Jane glanced at Elizabeth, silently pleading for assistance. Elizabeth had not told Jane about Georgiana's near elopement. That had been a Darcy secret she was not free to share.

However, Jane simply saw the best in everyone. She would not be able to doubt Will solely by virtue of who she was. Mary, on the other hand, had no such prejudices.

"I am not at liberty to speak about it," Elizabeth said. "However, Miss Darcy does deserve her brother's censure. I knew when she suggested the idea that we separate that Will would not approve. However, I am not her mother or her guardian, and I cannot insist or make her obey. Indeed, she is at an age where nobody can. All Will can do is offer consequences for disobedience in hopes she learns to make the correct decisions."

"But you only know what he has told you."

"This is true, but I trust him. Believe me, he would have no reason to lie. If it appears he is harsh with his sister, it is nothing compared to how he blames himself. I assure you, he only wants what is best for her. As none of us have ever had to raise a sixteen-year-old sister, I would say we do not have the right to have an opinion."

"But Papa is never so strict, and we have all turned out fine."

"Papa trusts us, and we have earned that trust. Miss Darcy has broken Will's and that is all there is to say about it."

Mary said nothing more but stabbed the fabric in an angry manner, as though she were biting her tongue and willing herself not to speak further. Her loyalty to Miss Darcy shocked Elizabeth. Jane and Elizabeth exchanged a glance. They would discuss it later. For now, they looked forward to the arrival of their suitors.

A few minutes later, Will and Charles arrived. It thrilled Elizabeth's heart to see unabashed joy enter Jane's eyes at Charles' arrival. His grin matched her intense feelings exactly, and after a quick greeting, he excused himself to Mr. Bennet's study. Mary glared at Will for a few minutes before giving some reason to leave.

"Your cousin did not come?" Elizabeth asked once Mary was gone.

"No, he was needed with his regiment. You may guess why Georgiana was not invited."

"Indeed," Elizabeth nodded. "I am sorry she is behaving so poorly. If we did not have enough worries with Wickham, I would find more compassion for her. I know it will soon be my place."

Will sighed. "If she continues to treat you with such disrespect, I will not have her in our homes. She is welcome to stay with Richard's mother. The countess asks after her often. Perhaps I ought to have allowed her to be raised by one of my aunts. However, Father left her in my care, and I did not wish to send her away. She had disliked going to school so much that I did not think making her live with relations would be any better."

"The poor dear has gone through very much," Jane said.

Elizabeth agreed. "I do not like her behaviour, but it could have very easily have been Jane or me acting that way. I know Sam thought I was full headstrong when I declared my love for you."

"You think I have been wrong about Wickham?" Will eyed her with bewilderment.

"No! Of course not." Elizabeth shook her head. "However, I understand the sentiments of a lady her age believing herself to be in love. If Father had not remarried, and if Sam were much older than me and I did not have dear Jane, then I might have very well turned into something resembling her."

"You do not blame me?" Will asked looking at his hands and Elizabeth perceived he was too afraid to meet her eyes. "I have thought over it and cannot think of a time when she was spoiled or not held to consequences. Perhaps I was too harsh on her—"

Elizabeth placed a hand on Will's knee, which bounced during his speech. "Dearest, you are not to blame. You have done the best you can. Was she always so difficult? I do not remember her being this way a few years ago."

"No," Will shook his head. "She returned from Ramsgate spewing venom, but I never would have allowed her to go if she had behaved like this. I am surprised that a few weeks around Wickham could have her reacting this way so much later, but then I learned he had frequently visited her without my knowledge."

"I do not understand it any better than you," Elizabeth said with an encouraging smile. "However, none of us are frozen in time and cease to develop and change. Somehow, she will move on from this, and in a year or two's time we can look back and sigh in relief."

"I suppose you are correct. I have learned the value of patience." Will sighed. "Now, I should tell you about my meeting with Colonel Forster."

"I assume it was not successful or you would have led with that."

"It was not as successful as I had wished," Will acknowledged. "Wickham is in the militia but has behaved above reproach. There is nothing I could say that would persuade the colonel to treat Wickham differently than the other officers. I could not explain about Georgiana, and stories about how he spent his inheritance too freely made little impression."

"I recall him being friends with Lord Harcourt," Elizabeth said slowly. Still, the thought of the detestable lord made her skin crawl. "I thought Wickham gambled heavily. Does he not have debts?"

Will shook his head. "None that I am aware of. I could have Richard investigate about London, but I know he was not in debt in Lambton."

"How did he live after spending the three thousand pounds from you?"

"I know not. When he made his application for the living in Kympton, he did not mention bad living situations, and I had supposed he lived off the interest of what I gave him. Wickham always had expensive tastes, but I assumed he had learned to moderate them lest he exceed his income. Just because he realised he did not prefer to study the law does not mean he had spent all of the money."

"I see," Elizabeth said and bit her bottom lip. "What is your next plan?"

Will tensed and did not immediately reply.

"Will?"

"Before leaving, Richard came up with a possible method of ascertaining Wickham's plans. He is an accomplished military strategist, and his suggestion was a very common practice."

Elizabeth turned to her sister. "Jane, would you excuse us a moment?"

"I am not supposed to leave." Jane looked conflicted.

"Fear not, I will not be sacrificing my honour."

"Your honour?" Jane and Will asked in unison.

"Will's reputation shall be perfectly safe with me," Elizabeth grinned.

"Very well," Jane sighed and stood up. She hesitated at the door, but left Will and Elizabeth alone.

The second the door closed, Elizabeth turned to her betrothed. "Tell me."

"Did you really send your sister away so you might question me? Did you think I had qualms about stating my plans before her?"

"Oh, no," Elizabeth gave Will a sly look. "I merely assured our privacy for later."

"Later?"

"After you tell me your plan, of course." Elizabeth raised her brows.

Will let out an exhale, and his eyes drifted to her mouth. "That was quite a wager. I did not think you were the gambling sort."

"Indeed, I am not," Elizabeth leaned closer and Will's breath quickened. "I have long admired your logical mind and how you make use of our time," she murmured near his ear. She glanced at the clock then pulled back. Sitting demurely in her seat, she allowed a finger to trace a circle on Will's knee. "However, if you prefer, we could spend the few minutes of privacy we have speaking about the weather, your sister, or—"

"Enough, woman!" Will clutched her to him, and Elizabeth let out a surprised yelp. With his mouth hovering over hers, he confessed, "Wickham has waited years to make his move. He will only do so under certain conditions. However, he showed his desires, and now we can pretend to give him what he wants."

Will met Elizabeth's lips, and for a moment, she gave into the kiss. However, her brain had not stopped operating despite his best efforts. She pushed him back. "Will, are you saying that you plan on baiting Wickham?"

"Yes." He trailed kisses down her throat as his hands wandered across her back.

Focusing all of her attention on his words, and not his heavenly ministrations, Elizabeth attempted again. "You would never endanger someone else. Who will you use?"

Will nuzzled into where her neck met her shoulder. The effect was dizzying. Elizabeth began to consider he would beat her at her own game. "Will?"

He kissed across her collarbone and up the other side of her throat before finding the sensitive spot near her ear. Thinking he had not heard her, she shook his shoulder a little. "Are you putting yourself in danger with this plan?"

Will then met Elizabeth's lips in a crushing kiss, stealing all thought for a moment. It was not more than they had shared before, but certainly more openly—in her family's drawing room! The thought brought her mind back to the present. He was avoiding this conversation. She could not blame him; she had provided the tools for it. This time she pushed him away and dodged his lips when he attempted to kiss her again.

"Will, do not tell me that you are to be the lure." When he did not answer, she cried, "Answer me!"

"Which do you prefer? That I answer you or that I do not tell you that I will be the bait?"

Elizabeth gasped and felt as though she had been slapped. The headiness of their previous kisses was now gone. "You would put yourself in harm's way? Why? Do I mean nothing to you?"

"You mean everything to me!" Will said and raised her hands to his lips. "We could think of no other way to make him take his mark."

Elizabeth could hear no more. Tearing her hands from his grasp, she ran from the room, sobbing.

Chapter Seven

"Young man," Mr. Bennet stood in the open doorway, bringing Will's attention to it. "Follow me, if you please."

Will followed the patriarch to his library, knowing the rebuke his betrothed's father would be giving him. Will sat opposite Mr. Bennet and patiently waited for the older man to begin.

"Will, I tire of seeing my daughter with tears in her eyes because of you." Mr. Bennet sighed.

"It shreds my heart as well," Will agreed. "Are you rescinding your blessing?" The papers had been signed but had not been mailed to his solicitor yet.

"And have her angry with me, as well?" Bennet laughed. "No, but we must resolve this latest complication as fast as possible. What is your plan? I can assume it must be foolish and reckless to upset Lizzy so."

Will blew out the breath he had been holding. "If Wickham wants to kill me, then we have the surest chance of capturing him if he feels assured of his success. He does not know that his plan with the carriage almost worked. It is likely he will attempt such a scheme again."

"So, you will endanger your life?"

"I see no other way."

Suddenly, the door to the library banged open. Turning to see the intruder, Will's heart seized to see Elizabeth standing in the doorframe with puffy eyes and tear streaks on her cheeks. She held a crumpled paper in her hand. A determined glint was in her eyes, but she gently shut the door before saying her piece. Once the door was closed, she sailed forward and demurely sat in a chair near her father's desk before addressing them both.

"It is not the only way. This may be indelicate for me to suggest, but how does Wickham hold his liquor?"

"It was many years ago when we were last in company," Will began to answer. "However, even when in his cups he seemed more in control of his faculties than others such as—"

"Such as Sam," Elizabeth answered and nodded. "One night while we stayed at Darcy House, I found him in a drunken state and unable to open his chamber door. The drink had made him quite chatty. I did not understand all that he was saying then, but now I know he was explaining his regret over the engagement with Charlotte Lucas."

"What are you suggesting?" Mr. Bennet asked.

"Ply him with drink and see if he will spill his secrets," Elizabeth said with furrowed brows and pleading eyes.

"Do you think that will work?" Bennet asked Will.

"I doubt it," Will shook his head. "Forgive me, love. It is very innovative, and I dare say on many another man it would work. However, I have never seen Wickham talk when he preferred to be silent."

"Is it not worth trying?" Elizabeth approached and laid a hand on Will's arm. Anguish filled her eyes and tears threatened to overspill once more. "At least attempt this before you risk your life."

Will gulped and slowly nodded. "We will try it," he murmured.

Truthfully, he had little hope of success, but how could he not offer her this balm? Will had spent years wishing he had done something differently the night of the fire in Scotland. He might have saved his father and friends' lives. If Elizabeth had an alternative, no matter how confident he was of its failure, he would allow her the opportunity to see it in motion. If anything happened to him, he did not wish for her to feel as though they had not done everything else possible.

"You will?" Elizabeth's voice contained a mixture of disbelief and relief. Her shoulders sagged and she let out a long exhale.

"How shall you manage that?" Mr. Bennet asked.

"We will have to have someone else approach him. He would be far too guarded if it were me or anyone associated with us. We can probably find somebody willing to get drunk for a few pounds."

"Keep me apprised of your plans, please," Mr. Bennet said, nodding at Will.

"Papa, may I speak with Will privately?"

"Very well," Bennet stood. "However, the door stays open."

Will did not even pay attention to Elizabeth's father as he left the room. His eyes were focused entirely on his betrothed. The minute he said they would try her plan, he became entranced. Would she always have this hold over him? He was utterly fascinated and captivated by the many sides of her. At the moment, she held his gaze with softened eyes. What had he ever done to deserve the look of love he saw there? He had thrown away her love when she first offered it. Since his return into her life, they had quarreled and feared for their lives. They desperately needed a routine courtship. A part of Will knew, however, they would not get it. He would simply court her after they married.

"What changed your mind?"

Will shrugged. "I love you. This concerns you just as much as it does me. You have a stake in the matter, and your idea should be listened to."

"Is that all?"

"I could sense how desperately you wanted to try this method. I do not wish to lie, Elizabeth. I think it unlikely that it will succeed. However, not only does it make sense to try it, I knew it would assuage some of your anxiety." Will dropped his head for a moment and took a deep breath before bringing his eyes and back up to meet her gaze. "I know what it is to be haunted by remorse and regret, constantly feeling as though you might have done something different to prevent catastrophe. I would not put you through that. If you have any other suggestions, I will hear them out, and we will attempt them. If the worse should happen—"

"Hush, my love." Elizabeth placed a finger on Will's lips to silence them. "Do not speak about that. Do not even think it. We shall be victorious.

I believe that with every beat of my heart. Thank you for agreeing to my suggestion."

Elizabeth lowered her hand and turned the crumpled paper over on her lap for a moment. Her eyes lingered over the note before returning to Will's. "I am very sorry to hear that you have regret and feel as though you could have prevented something happening. Do I understand that you reference the fire?"

Will could not speak, the emotions threatened to well up once more. He nodded and knew that would be enough for Elizabeth.

"Has it helped at all to know that it was arson? If you had been with your father or Sam, you could not have prevented the fire. A madman was determined to set fire to the inn that night. If you had been with them, you probably would have perished as well."

Will blinked at what Elizabeth said. Suddenly awe and understanding flitted through him, and a weight the size of a house lifted from his shoulders. "I had not thought of that. I have been so consumed with blaming myself that I did not even consider it in that light." Will enveloped Elizabeth's hands in his. "Thank you, my dearest. You always know what to say."

Elizabeth lightly chuckled. "I would not go that far." Her soft smile began to fade, and she grew serious once more. "No matter the cause of the fire, it would not have been your fault they died. Accidents happen, and there is no one to blame. However, I am pleased if what I said brought some comfort to you. I hate that you have blamed yourself and felt wretched for so long. Why do you do it? Why do you think everything is your responsibility and that if the smallest thing goes wrong, you have failed? You are only human."

Will's eyes shuttered closed at Elizabeth's words. "You did not see much of my father. He was a very good man, but he had high expectations for the Darcy family. The ways of charm and grace did not come naturally to me, so I often felt inexplicably flawed and doomed to failure, unable to live up to the Darcy legacy."

"I see," Elizabeth nodded. "So continuing to accept only perfection from yourself has eased those feelings?"

"No. I suppose not." Will furrowed his brow. "The Darcy legacy demands the best. With me at the helm, it feels as though it has gone through one blunder after another."

"One blunder after another? I suppose your tenants are starving and their roofs caving in?

Your servants are owed money or have left en masse? You have no friends and no admittance to any events wherever you go. You have debts at every shop in every town you ever visited, and no creditor would allow your entrance to his establishment."

A small slowly crept over Will's face. "Fair enough, clever minx. None of those things are true. I know I do very fine by the Darcy accounts. The Darcy name is as strong as ever it was during my father's lifetime and it continues to command respect. However, I failed to save my father's life, I failed you, and I failed Georgiana."

Once more, Elizabeth silenced him with a finger to his lips. "Do you not see? All those things revolve around other people's choices. You cannot control everything, Will Darcy. I am pleased to hear that the accounts do well, you are wise with investments, and others continue to respect you. However, even those things do not rely entirely on your actions. Do not judge yourself by the success of this or that. Those things do not determine your worth."

"Are not most people given to arrogance and conceit? Would not most people fail to inspect themselves and admit when they have done wrong?"

Elizabeth nodded. "I suppose you could say that. However, thinking you have done wrong where there is no responsibility is just as terrible."

"How so?"

"For some, that would only be false modesty and really would be an indirect boast. 'I have done so terribly,' and then their friend will say 'no, you have not,' and inwardly the person will congratulate themselves. I know those are not your feelings. No, yours speak to hurt and insecurity. When you continue to feed that feeling, it will infect more and more facets of your life. Right now, it is mostly centered on Wickham, but it has affected your relationship with me in the past. You admit that you never told Georgiana about the scoundrel. I know your relationship with her at the moment is not what you would like it to be, and perhaps you cannot fully expose what Wickham is to her, for she will not listen. Again, that relies on her as well as you. However, if you interpret everything as a failure in those situations, you will tell yourself that is all you are. You will lack the confidence you need to make wise decisions on other matters."

"I do not think I have ever heard such things before. I certainly have never considered them. How wise and right you are, my love. Thank you. I shall try to do better." Will looked down at Elizabeth's hands; she continued to finger the note she held. "Is that my message to you from yesterday?"

Elizabeth looked down as well. "Yes. With all the excitement, I did not have a chance to read it. When I left you in the drawing room and ran up to my chamber, I noticed it on the table. How I ever garnered your attention, I do not know. I am forever grateful for it, though. Reading your words of love, your devotion to me and to the future we will build, allowed me to see the reason behind your choice. You did not suggest baiting Wickham because you have no desire to be with me or just to shorten your life. You have only wanted to end this so we might have our future at last. Once my mind was clear, I recalled the situation with Sam and knew that I could suggest the idea to you. I did not know if you would agree to it. Nor do I want you to do so merely out of deference. However, I was unable to think of it in the drawing room. All was doom and gloom in my head until I read your loving words."

Will squeezed Elizabeth's hands again before raising them to his lips. He would have liked for much more but was conscious of the fact that they had been alone for quite a while, even if the door was open. "I meant every word. I will love you until my dying breath. Now, I believe we should join your family. There ought to be congratulations in order."

“Do you mean he has—?” Elizabeth’s hands flew to her mouth to contain a squeal of delight. “Oh, Jane will be delighted!”

“Yes, Charles has asked your father for courtship with Jane.”

“Well, it is about time. Although,” Elizabeth slid Will a sly glance. “I suppose not everyone is as rapid to the altar as we.”

“Considering that when I proposed five years ago, I expected a marriage within months, I would say we have taken quite the adventurous route to get to it.”

“It will make us enjoy the moment all the more.”

“I know I shall.” Will raised Elizabeth’s hands to his lips before allowing himself to be escorted to the drawing room.

Chapter Eight

In the drawing room the following morning Will arrived while Elizabeth sat with Jane and Mary.

"Will," Elizabeth said in astonishment. "I did not expect you until later." She took in the severe frown he wore. "Is anything wrong?"

"Forgive me," he said. "I thought this matter could not wait until later."

He said nothing else and Elizabeth looked at her sisters. "Would you like me to ask for them to leave?"

"No, for it is your sister with whom I need to speak."

"Me?" Jane asked. "Oh, no! Is something wrong with Charles? Is he ill?"

"Charles is very well. It is your sister Mary with whom I wish to talk."

Elizabeth looked at her younger sister. She noted Mary did not seem surprised.

"Yes, sir? How may help you?" Mary continued her sewing, without looking up.

"Did you meet with my sister yesterday?"

"Indeed, yes."

"Did she not mention to you that she was not to leave the house?"

"No, sir, she did not. I went for a walk and happened upon her between here and Netherfield. It hardly would have occurred to me that she had been out walking without permission." She stabbed her needle into the fabric and drew the thread through it before continuing. "Just as it hardly would have occurred to me that she needed such."

Elizabeth gasped. "Mary! You will keep your opinions about Will and Miss Darcy to yourself."

"She may as well tell me what Georgiana has poisoned her mind with, my love. Then I will know some of the imaginary complaints my sister has against me."

They all stared at Mary in expectation who had looked up but blinked with uncertainty at the scrutiny.

"Upon my word, Miss Darcy has said nothing against you, sir. She did not claim that it was harsh of you to demand she stay home. She did not tell me that had been your demand at all." She blew out a breath. "Either you mistake her sentiments, or she did not understand your request. If she had wanted to make me think ill of you, she could have told me about your imperious rules. However, she did not. I think ill of you by my own observation."

"I see," Will said. "What else have you observed?"

"I have not known Georgiana for long. However, she seems the type of girl who is eager to please. She wants to be well-liked, and she craves independence. Surely a girl of her age, maturity, and experience in the world would understand the only way to gain independence is by earning your trust. Therefore she should be endeavoring to earn yours. That you have not given it says far more about you than her."

Elizabeth scoffed and exchanged a look of confused amazement with her betrothed. What ridiculous reasoning her sister had!

"When I return to Netherfield, I will continue to make even clearer to Georgiana what my expectations are. She is not allowed to leave the house without an escort. As you have determined to become her friend, I have now made you aware of my expectation, as well. In a few weeks, Miss Mary, I will be marrying your sister. That will make Elizabeth a sister to my own. However, you do not receive such rights by blood or law upon the marriage. You have proved to me, her guardian, that you are not a worthwhile friend and someone I can trust to influence my sister appropriately."

Mary's mouth fell open and her eyes watered. "Do you see, Lizzy? Do you see? I wonder how you can marry such a brute!"

Mary ran out of the room, dropping her sewing along the way and stifling a sob with a hand to her mouth. At a more sedate pace, Jane followed after her. Next, Will finally sat down in the chair next to Elizabeth. She frowned at him. While he had every right to say what he did, and she did not blame him for the sentiment, it was not well executed. Chastising Mary was not his responsibility. Nor had she done anything to earn his ire. It is not as though she insisted Georgiana leave the house or lied when questioned about it.

Additionally, sometimes being too harsh had the opposite effect of what one intended. Mary had always been an obedient child; no one had ever raised a voice to her. Will leaned forward and rested his elbows on his knees. He sighed so heavily, it sounded as though the weariness came from his bones. Elizabeth watched as Will first rubbed at his temples and then squeezed the bridge of his nose. This ordeal was giving him a headache and must have weighed heavily on him. The last thing he needed was a rebuke from Elizabeth.

"Would you like me a call for some powders?" Elizabeth whispered.

"Thank you, no, my love. I shall be well in a moment."

Elizabeth sat in silence as Will attempted to rid himself of his pain. She wished she could see to his needs the way a wife would. If they were already married, she would have overruled him. He would be consuming powders and tea while lying in a cool, dark room as she massaged his temples. However, such things were far too intimate for her to do right now. She had never before considered the difficulty in seeing a loved one in such pain and being unable to assist them. Tea soon arrived, and Elizabeth smiled as she poured Will's cup. Jane must have sent it. Thankfully, the beverage soon returned him to good humor.

"What happened after you left Longhorn yesterday?" Elizabeth asked.

Will shook his head. "As Charles and I were returning to the stables, we saw Georgiana ascending the stairs to the house. I questioned her, and for quite some time, she refused to say anything. Finally, she spoke, but the most I got out of her was that she had seen your sister Mary."

"I see," she said. "Why did you not send a note last night?"

"By the time Georgiana said anything at all it was nearing suppertime. I was exhausted from the experience and thought it would be better to question Mary in person today."

"And yet just now it did not seem like you were calm when you entered the room."

"No." Will shook his head. "No, I was not. I slept ill, thinking of all the danger that might have befallen her. I cannot get it out of my head that Wickham has twisted her mind somehow and is using her against me."

"Do you think she would be willing to do that? Does she hate you so much?"

"I hope not." Will sighed and ran a hand over his face. "I cannot think of what I have done to make her so angry with me; so willing to believe Wickham's words. However, he did visit her when I was not around. Who knows how he poisoned her for years?"

"However, she did not act out until recently, correct?" Elizabeth asked.

"That is correct. She seemed as loving and devoted as ever until Ramsgate."

Elizabeth had no answers for Will. She did not understand her soon-to-be sister-in-law's mind any better than he did. Additionally, she had not been around for the years in between. She also could not understand Mary's resentment toward Will. But then, her mother's and Charlotte's hatred of him did not make sense to Elizabeth, either. Perhaps grief affected everyone strangely. It is not as though she had only kind thoughts of Will during the years they had been separated. They sat in silence for several minutes with Elizabeth only holding his hand. At last, an idea struck her. "What if Wickham is using Georgiana, although not in the way you suppose?"

"What do you mean?"

"What if he intends to merely distract you with all these issues with Georgiana so you cannot focus on him?"

"That is a possibility, I suppose. What do you suggest?"

"When you return to Netherfield, list very firm and clear rules for Georgiana. She cannot leave without an escort, as an example. Explain what the consequences to such misbehavior would be. Being sent to Pemberley or London might not be much of a deterrent," Elizabeth observed. "What would she wish to avoid?

"This reminds me so very much of a conversation I have had with Charles recently. However, Georgiana is not spoiled as Caroline is. Loss of funds would not be a strong deterrent. Other than shopping with you and your sisters the other day, she had not gone in months. I could send her away." Will stroked his jaw. "She is fond of our aunt, the countess. However, Georgiana does not like staying in their home. They have far too many engagements during the Season for her liking. I can always send her to Lady Catherine, but given how she sent Collins to you in an attempt for me to marry her daughter, I do not wish to speak to her."

Elizabeth nodded. "Those give us a direction in which to start. We may think of others later. Lay down these rules and then do not give her any more attention, except to praise her obedience."

"I am not to correct her when she does wrong again?"

"That is up to you. I suppose you could give her one chance. However, do not make a game of it where she feels she holds your attention or consumes your thoughts." Elizabeth refilled her tea and looked over her shoulder. Jane had not reentered, but the door was open. "Now, have you considered how to approach the scheme of getting Wickham drunk?"

"I have had little time to consider it. Have you?"

"I did entertain some thoughts last night. I will tell them to you, and you may improve them as needed."

As it happened, Elizabeth's plan did not need improvement. Will returned to Netherfield ready to make his sister see reason. Later, he would have to apologize for losing his temper with Miss Mary. He called for a servant to send for Georgiana, Mrs. Annesley, and Charles to be brought the drawing room.

"Fitzwilliam," Georgiana said with a scowl. "Why have you requested me? I am sure whatever you have to say cannot apply to both Mr. Bingley and me."

Will scowled again at his sister's words. It should no longer surprise, and yet it continued to do so. "I have asked Charles here so he could also witness this and avoid any possibility of confusion with any person staying in this house."

"What? And is Mr. Bingley to be my master now?" Georgiana said.

"I have conferred with Miss Mary Bennet, and she says she stumbled upon you while out walking. She says you never told her you were not to leave the house. She thinks my instructions were not clear enough. Allow me to rectify that now. Georgiana, you are confined to the house—not the grounds—the house, unless you have an escort. Nor does this mean bullying Mrs. Annesley into anything. Do you understand?"

"What counts as an escort? May I ride if the groom attends me? May I shop if a manservant or maid is present?"

Will thought for a moment. "Most of the time, I will prefer that you leave in the company of me, Charles, or Mrs. Annesley. There may be times, however, where I will allow you to leave or go with another. However, you must earn it and prove that you will not abuse the situation. As such, I would suggest you not attempt or hope for it for several weeks."

Georgiana rolled her eyes in disgust.

"Is that clear enough for you, Georgiana?" Will stared at his sister.

"Why should I bother at all? Lock me in a tower. We both know that is what you would prefer. I am far too much in the way of your plans to woo Miss Elizabeth. I suppose this takes immediate effect?"

"Certainly. Can you comply? No. I should not ask that question. I know you are perfectly capable."

"You know nothing about what I am capable of," Georgiana glared at her brother. "You know nothing about me. You never have and you never will."

"I see. I have forgotten a crucial element of this meeting," Will said.

"What is that?"

"Should you not comply, you will be sent away."

"That does not surprise me. After all, you convinced Mr. Bingley to do so to Caroline."

"Miss Darcy," Charles said in a shockingly angry voice. "You are a guest in my house, and as such you must display certain manners towards your brother and me. Your brother did not convince me of anything. Caroline's actions warranted the decision."

"Thank you, Charles," Will said. "Georgiana, if you do not comply with these requests, I will be forced to send you to one of our aunts. If that does not work, then I will send you to a reformatory school."

"A reformatory school!" Georgiana looked at her brother as though he had three heads. "That is where girls of ill repute go! You cannot do that to me. I am a Darcy, and I have noble blood just as much as you do. The earl and the countess would not care for that and neither would Lady Catherine, you know."

"It would not matter whether they like it or not. As your guardian, I make the decision. It would pain me to do so. However, I would do plenty worse rather than continue to make excuses for your behavior and not correct them. You are influenced by a man with no credibility. He has made more errors than you can conceive. It began, I am sorry to say, when our father did not accept the truth of him. Indeed, it would be more comfortable for me to pretend such things never occurred. But they did, and I have spent far too long acting as though they had no influence over the present. You made a mistake to trust Mr. Wickham. It is not too late to change your course. I also made the mistake of listening to him. Unlike you, I did not like or even respect him. I did so, and it had lasting and devastating consequences. It separated me from the woman I love. She needed me and my support for years."

Tears shimmered in Georgiana's eyes when Will had finished, but they did not appear to be tears of sadness or remorse. Will had a sinking feeling everything he just said meant nothing to her, as though she never heard him all. Later, he told himself, he would take the time to worry about his sister's path and question how they could correct it. For now, his concern had to be seeing to her safety and also the protection of Elizabeth. "Now, if you agree to these terms, you may return to your room. I must speak to Charles privately."

As expected, Georgiana said nothing. She stood and held her head high as she left the room. She did not stomp her feet, but her feelings were clear all the same. Mrs. Annesley followed after her. Will motioned for Charles to follow him and they retreated to the study. After closing the door, Will let out a long sigh.

"And this is why I never took the trouble to check Caroline all these years. As terribly difficult as it must be for you now, I wish I had done so with my sister long ago. I do not know if I can ever have her in my homes again. I will not abide mistreatment of Jane or the Bennets. However, Hurst tells me she is of a mind to marry. As such, I do not know that she will ever learn the intended lesson."

"Our tactics may be similar, Charles, but our motivations are different. Miss Bingley may never learn to be kind to Jane and the Bennets. However, she will learn where your boundaries are and what lines she can and cannot cross with you.

"This is true. So, if we have different motivations regarding our sisters, what then is yours?"

"I hardly know. I would wish for the return of the sweet girl she was not so long ago. In my heart, I do not know if that is possible."

"No, indeed. We all have experiences in life which change us, and we cannot go back to who we were before. But do not give up on her, Darcy. Now, what did you wish to talk to me about?"

Will gave his friend a small smile. "Thank you for your support, Charles. You have always been a good friend. You put up with me when most others would tell me to sot my arrogant self off."

Charles laughed. "I have been sorely tempted at times."

Will laughed as well. Charles then listened attentively as Will explain Elizabeth's proposal. "Do you have such a man we could use?"

"There is one I would consider. I think Evans might do. His aunt heard of this position and sent for him. I understand he spent many years in Manchester, and wished for a new lease on life. Caroline wanted me to let him go because he did not seem to have the proper look and mannerisms for a footman, in her opinion. However, he gets his work done, and my housekeeper has no complaints."

"Excellent," Will nodded. "Send him tomorrow. Now, I must write a note of apology to Miss Mary for my sharp questioning of her. She gave me a set down, as was needed."

"Did she really? I might have gotten the only docile sister of the bunch!" Charles laughed. He stood and walked to the door, but spoke over his shoulder before opening. "I do hope Elizabeth's scheme works. There can be only so many dour men in the world, I should hate to have to find a new one to make friends with."

Will laughed as Charles left him to his devices. Charles had been a good friend and if the positions were reversed, Will probably would call him stupid for attempting such a thing and volunteered in his place. With any luck, Wickham would get drunk tomorrow and fill in all the details. Then Will would put this matter behind him and carry on with his engagement.

Chapter Nine

Will and Charles consumed their supper the following evening in silence, Mrs. Annesley and Georgiana having already retired to their rooms. An ungentlemanly case of nerves caused their disquiet. This evening, Charles's footman would attempt to get Wickham drunk in the Meryton tavern. Will had spoken to the young man, and he needed minimal coaching the play the sort of person Wickham would feel most comfortable around: an easy mark in cards and a drunken lightweight with just enough money for Wickham to win a few pounds. Will had once heard Wickham tell Sam to be careful of playing with the wealthy or titled. At the time, Will thought that showed unusual insight on Wickham's behalf, before determining it only meant Wickham had learned those gentlemen did not always honor their debts, and men such as he were powerless to call their honor into question.

It had rained all day, making a visit to Longbourn impossible. Will and Charles consoled their troubled minds and lonely hearts with dull rounds of billiards. At last, the evening came, and Evans was sent on his way. It was after midnight when he returned. The servant was brought to Charles's library.

"Well, man?" Charles asked after Evans had consumed a liberal amount of coffee to sober himself.

Will held his breath. Until this moment, he had not realized that he had begun to hope. He had not thought the plan would work. He told himself it could not, so he ought not to expect it. Will wryly mused to himself that by now, he ought to be used to his heart deciding whatever it wished, regardless of his determination.

"He barely tasted a drop all night," Evans said.

"What?" Charles cried.

"I suspected he could hold his liquor well," Will said with an annoyed sigh. "I had not thought he would resist entirely."

"It was not until the other men accused him of being a Methodist or a teetotaler that he drank more than a sip or two of his pint. At that point, I was at such a disadvantage that although he paid for several rounds, there was no getting him drunk."

Will stroked his jaw in thought. Growing up, his father had told him never to overindulge, especially in a business meeting. Wickham had often heard same advice. Did he feel he had a reason to be on guard and keep his head clear at the tavern? Had he suspected their plan? No one knew of it—even Georgiana. She was upstairs during the conversation and Evans was not asked until just before he left to perform the duty. Will sighed. The truth was, the tactic was probably too obvious. They might have had better luck hoping to bribe one of Wickham's usual drinking fellows. Of course, they then ran the risk of the man being loyal to Wickham and not keeping the secret. "Did you speak with any other people present? Did anyone remark on his usual habits?"

"Aye," said Evans. "One or two of them said they never saw him drink. A few others acknowledged that he never drank to excess. Although, he would sometimes buy rounds for others when in a particularly good mood and spent much of his free time in the establishment."

"It seemed like he was a fixture there?" Charles asked.

"More so than other officers," the footman answered.

"How curious," Charles observed.

"Someone told me he was regarded as the most alert officer Colonel Forster had."

"Very interesting," Will answered. "Thank you, that will be all."

Charles pressed a coin or two into the young man's hand before he left the room. Charles shut the door, then turned to his companion. "Well? "Do you want to try again? Perhaps we could bribe one of his cronies—"

Will interrupted, "I do not think that will work. I had considered it, as well. Considering Wickham's mission, he must think it best not to dull his senses. Unlike his colleagues, he cannot afford to relax when his shift is over. I wonder at his diligence, however. If his intention really is to wound or kill me, then why must he worry about relaxing in the tavern? I would never frequent the place. Surely he would want stealth and an alibi on his side when he perpetrates the act."

"I do not doubt that," Charles said. "If he were here with the intention to blackmail you, again, he would not need to be alert in the tavern. If he were merely here on duty, he would behave as his other officers."

Will shook his head. "I cannot make sense of it. If he wished to wound me by hurting Georgiana or Elizabeth, there would be no reason to be concerned at a tavern. In fact, he would be spending less time there and would surely attempt to meet the ladies while they were in a shop or out walking. Forster says that he is a model officer and is always present at duty. He would only have free time in the evening, when they are not shopping. On the other hand, he does not go to the events other officers are invited to. It is unlike Wickham not to crave superior company."

The gentlemen sat in silence for another moment. Will continued to mull over the report, and he suspected Charles did, as well. When the clock struck half past, they decided to get some sleep. Perhaps things would be more evident in the morning.

Unfortunately, the morning did not bring clarity to matters. It continued to rain, separating Will and Elizabeth. As he could not speak to her in person, he wrote a letter, knowing she would not be pleased to read his words.

Dear Elizabeth,

I wish, my darling, that I could convey better news. Not only did we not learn any crucial information from Wickham last night, but our informant also claims that he barely touched any alcohol. Further reports from his colleagues and locals make it clear that Wickham will over-indulge for no one while here. I am afraid this way of thinking is at an end. Your plan was well-thought out, and I am pleased you suggested it. I wish it had succeeded and take no enjoyment from its failure.

How I hate this rain which keeps us apart! What was I thinking of, purchasing a common license? If I had spent the money on a special license, we could call the minister to your house whenever we pleased—and I would be well-pleased to marry you this instant—and then we would never be separated again. However, I do not doubt that in a fortnight we will wed, and a more beautiful bride there will never be on this earth. Regardless of matters with Wickham, I will meet you at that church and promise to love, honour, and cherish you. I have in thought for many years and soon will show you every day. Do you long for the day we are husband and wife as I do?

I know you must be afraid for the next plan we have considered. I see no other way. There is naught to be done but to be brave and have faith. As soon as I can, I will be acting upon it, and I trust when we next meet that all shall be over and we will triumph in victory.

Until then, remember my love for you. My memory is dotted with the exquisite torture of your gentle caresses and passionate kisses. I pray you have the same. May the remembrance of them steal your breath as you feel as though my arms are wrapped around you, and our hearts beat in unison. In the quiet moments of your day, hear the whisper of my heart: I love you until the end of my days. Always and forever, you are my only love.

-Will

Will looked over his letter as a nervous flutter filled his heart. He was full of bravado in his message, but he could not ignore the possibility that he might never see Elizabeth again. The acknowledgment that he might never taste her lips another time nearly had him calling for his horse. Perhaps he could visit Longbourn before the carriage ride which would determine his fate.

No, he shook his head. The plan was for him to suddenly leave Netherfield in the direction of London. He and Richard had arranged for there to be scouts every few miles, hidden well off the road. They would await his arrival at a set time, and if he did not come, they would investigate. The hope was that if Wickham did attack, Will would not be without help for too long, and if he were wounded, there would be hope of help arriving in time. He had not explained this portion to Elizabeth, and she had not asked. They silently agreed to not go into the details so she might worry less.

Looking at the rain falling, Will sighed to himself. There was another matter he had to deal with before he could hope to lure Wickham out. He had not spoken with Georgiana beyond the merest civilities since his visit to Longbourn the other day. If anything should happen to him, he did not want her living the rest of her life thinking he hated her and the last words they spoke were in a quarrel. He rang the bell and awaited the arrival of a servant. Then, he asked for his note to be taken to Longbourn and if his sister would like to play for him in the drawing room. Again, the fragile hope beat in his heart. He hoped she would. Perhaps not all would be lost between them.

Elizabeth smiled as she took Will's missive from the platter the servant held toward her. She knew the previous evening her plan would be enacted. It must contain good news! It simply must!

Until she began reading, the thought that the scheme might fail had not entered her mind. For the alternative meant... It did not bear thinking of it! Before Elizabeth read more than the second line, tears shrouded her vision, and her grip tightened on the paper. Conscious of the watchful eyes of her family, she fled the drawing room for the privacy and solitude of her chamber.

Flinging herself on her bed, she sobbed as though she had already heard the news of Will's demise. Her tears now envied the ones she shed upon Sam's death. Was Will even now foolishly calling for his carriage and hurtling himself toward Wickham's clutches?

A gentle knock interrupted Elizabeth's anxious thoughts. Jane slipped into the room and softly rubbed Elizabeth's back until her tears slowed.

"What does he say?" Jane asked quietly.

"Can you not guess?" Elizabeth asked as she pushed herself up on her elbows before moving to a sitting position.

Jane only nodded. "When?"

Elizabeth blinked at her sister's question. She had not finished reading Will's letter. She had leapt to the conclusion that he was now hoping to ensnare Wickham at his own game. Perhaps he had changed his mind! Maybe he saw the sense in being less courageous. After all, they had not determined what Wickham's motive was. There were times when Elizabeth could almost convince herself this was naught but a nightmare and Will was in no danger.

Taking a deep breath and wiping at her eyes, Elizabeth readied herself to read the rest of Will's note. She smoothed the crinkled paper, and he eyes devoured the words.

His loving words consoled but could not relieve. His ending was too much like a farewell—a final farewell! "I must go to him!" she exclaimed.

"You cannot!" Jane said and tugged on Elizabeth's hand. She had immediately stood upon her pronouncement and was ready to fly from the house that instant.

Jane led Elizabeth to the window, where she surveyed the outside. The rain had ceased to be a constant flow and now came in drips and dribbles, but the ground was too wet for walking. She would be caked in mud. "The carriage or—or—" Elizabeth gulped, "a horse?"

"There is too much mud," Jane said.

Slowly, Elizabeth nodded. Indeed, today it would be too dangerous for horses to brave the roads but soon—in a day or two at most—they would be drivable and then Will would hope to catch Wickham.

"How will it be done?" Jane asked as she looked over Elizabeth's shoulder at the letter she still held.

"I do not know," Elizabeth sighed. Wrapping her arms around herself, she walked back to the bed and sat upon it. "I did not ask for any particulars. I would rather not know the exact scenario so my mind can picture it with perfect detail."

"You are so fatalist! It is not like you to be so defeated!"

"And you are too optimistic! Our brother died—died!—at the lunatic's actions. How can I hope that Will is any different?"

"Do you think Wickham has some supernatural ability? Will knows his enemy's intentions and his probable method. Indeed, he knows he has an enemy. Sam never did. Do you not see how Will's knowledge is an asset? Do you not trust his ability to plan?"

Elizabeth's lips quirked but she could not entirely give in to the desire to smile. "I am certain he is a brilliant landlord and master. He is a loyal friend and a devoted lover. However, what does he know about subverting the tactics of a madman? Oh! I wish we could have kept the Runners involved but it has nothing to do with London. Will could have hired a guard, but he did not wish to alert Wickham to knowledge of his plan."

"I would think that would be quite expensive. I do not think even the Prince Regent has a standing guard at all times."

"Who would want to kill him? A brother? Who would want to be heir to the crown if they could? Is it not more trouble than it is worth? If history has taught us nothing, you are in dire jeopardy of losing your head either by the ax or from madness. No, no one can envy Prinny the way Wickham envies Will."

Jane let out a sad sigh and squeezed her sister's hand. "What will you do then?"

"Wait," Elizabeth said with a determined tone as she straightened her back. "I have waited for him once, and I can wait again. I shall also pray for sunshine."

"Do you not wish to delay his actions?"

"No!" Elizabeth said as she walked to the window and willed the clouds to break. "No, I would rather get it over with."

"There is the fierce Lizzy that I know," Jane wrapped her arms around her sister. "Now that you are in better humour, you should reply to his note. The servant waits for your answer."

Elizabeth nodded and settled at the small writing desk in their chamber as Jane left her alone. Pouring all of her love into words, Elizabeth filled three sheets front and back with expressions of tenderness and affection. Will should never doubt her devotion. She added that he should carry it in his coat pocket. If she were to imagine his arms around her, then he should allow her words to surround him. They would provide protection and shelter more than any armed guard ever could. Love would prevail, she was sure of it.

The rest of the day continued in listless activities. Mary was put out with the weather and scowled every time she crossed a window. At dinner, Mrs. Bennet reported that the "little girls" were quite wild with being cooped up due to the rain. Then, she recalled that they could not have been any worse than a young Elizabeth and Sam after being ill in bed for days. The evening closed with fond memories. It was the first time Mrs. Bennet had mentioned Sam in many years, and she even mentioned Will a time or two. Elizabeth hoped that meant her step-mother was softening toward her betrothed.

Elizabeth awoke to sunny skies the next day. She nearly faced the residual mud to walk to

Netherfield, and Mary had offered to go as far as Meryton with her, but their father refused. Elizabeth sighed. It was true, they should not be walking about when Wickham might be on the loose. Will sent another loving note, but was too busy with his plans to spare time for a visit.

Sunday dawned with more sunshine. The roads would be perfectly dry by the morrow. During her nighttime prayers, Elizabeth fervently beseeched the Almighty for protection of her beloved. She felt akin to Abraham when he was asked to sacrifice his longed-for son as a test of his faith. At every instant, Elizabeth half expected an archangel to appear and tell her she had prevailed and Will would be spared. That it did not happen made Elizabeth wonder if she should become a shepherdess. Against her will, she fell asleep that night dreaming of flocks of sheep.

She dressed the following day with trembling hands. There was no more delaying it. In the pit of her stomach, she knew this would be the day that Will would face Wickham. She could not bear to eat at breakfast. She consumed tea and watched fretfully at the window. Mary chided her lack of faith, and Jane worried about her constitution, between refusing food and pacing the rooms. Mrs. Bennet, shockingly, sensibly suggested occupation instead and had spent much of her time in the drawing room rather than in the nursery giving Kitty and Lydia their lessons.

By the afternoon, exhaustion crept in. Elizabeth had been convinced to sit in a chair and sip on more tea as tempting and flavourful, biscuits were waved before her. If anyone would leave her alone for more than half a moment, she was sure she would fall asleep from the exertion of it all.

At first, she did not hear the sound of hooves on the drive. Soon, the panicked rate at which they ran drew the notice of Mary as she sat near a window and read. Within seconds there was a flurry of activity. Mary's gasp almost muffled the sound of boots on the drive and banging on the door. Jane ran to it before a servant could answer, and Mr. Bingley's voice was heard in the hall. Time felt as though it slowed as Elizabeth's head turned in the direction of the door frame where he now stood with a hat in his hand, face pale, and unable to speak. Elizabeth's cup fell from her hand and shattered on the floor in a thousand pieces.

Chapter Ten

Will awoke when someone called his name, and there was a pounding on the carriage door.

"Mr. Darcy! Mr. Darcy! Do you live, sir?"

Will grunted at the noise, the effort and the sound making his head ache. Touching his fingers to his temple, he felt the stickiness of blood oozing from his head. Forcing his eyes opened, he looked around at his surroundings. His carriage was on its side, and he had fallen with it.

What had happened? All was going according to plan. They were some miles from Meryton when he had heard it—a gunshot rang out. The horses startled and the driver lost control. The carriage toppled and threw Will hard against its side. He quickly tested his bones—nothing was broken. He ached, but nothing fatal occurred.

"Mr. Darcy!"

Will did not recognise the voice. It must be one of the hired hands who were to wait at the posts.

What was the fate of his driver? Outside the carriage, he heard the shouts of several men.

"I am here," Will called out. "I live!"

"Over here!" The man outside cried, and Will heard several men approach. "Mr. Darcy, can you move to the door? We are going to try opening it again and hoisting you out."

"Yes," Will answered slowly. "Yes, I think I can do that."

His legs buckled under the exertion at first, but he forced himself up. The door finally opened, allowing much-needed sunshine and fresh air into the cabin. A large man hovered over the opening and spoke through the door. His voice was not the one who spoke a moment before.

"Just grab my hand then, sir." The man shifted to extend his arm into the cabin.

Will heard the walls of the carriage creak over his head. His eyes scanned for a place to put his feet or pull on for it would be much better to climb out than be lifted like some dainty woman. The entrance stood a foot or two above his head making it an awkward angle to pull himself out of. Spying the handle meant for assisting passengers in and out of the carriage, Will informed the men that he would not need their help. There was a jostling as the stout man clambered back down to the ground.

Grabbing the handle on the side, Will pulled on it as one hand gripped the outside of the carriage door. He gave a little hop and then lifted himself out. A simple enough procedure that took untold amounts of effort, as his body still shook from the experience. Once outside, the gathered men cheered.

The big fellow from earlier laughed. "We thought you was tiny like all them lords are!"

"Mind your mouth, Jem," the man from earlier said as he approached. "Sir, we caught the dastard." He motioned for two other burly men to bring the trembling culprit forward. "He is called Bradley."

"I had to do it! I swear! He said he'd kill me children iffin' I didn't!"

"Who?" Will asked.

"He never told me no name."

"You saw his face? You would know him again?"

"Aye, sir."

"What do you want us to do with him?" The man who seemed to be their leader asked.

"Keep him for now. We will have to call the magistrate. However," he hastened to add when Bradley protested, "we will inform him of the circumstances."

The primary hand jerked his head, and the perpetrator was led away. Now recovered from the shock of the accident, Will's heart sank to realize Wickham had sent another to do his bidding. He ought to have expected that.

"Thank you for your assistance, Mr. ?" Will asked with a raised brow.

"Name's Samuels, sir. No mister."

Will's lips twitched. It was as though Sam had watched over him. "Well, Samuels, have you seen Mr. Bingley?"

"The minute we knew you were alive, he jumped on his horse and ran off. Said something about telling your missus. He is also sending a doctor for the coachman's leg. 'Tis a miracle he lives."

Will nodded. Charles had gone to tell Elizabeth that he lived. Bless his friend!

"You'll be needing a horse to get back home, and we got an extra for you here."

"Thank you." Will acknowledged his thanks with a tip of his head. There was much left to clean up the scene and deal with the would-be assassin, but all of that could wait. “I trust you to see to this. Mr. Bingley will return shortly.”

Will mounted the proffered horse and raced to Longbourn. Arriving there, he dismounted and opened the door without knocking. He nearly tore it from the hinges. He got no more than a few steps into the house before Elizabeth ran and threw her arms around him. She must have been waiting for him in the hall after Charles told her of his accident.

“Will!” Elizabeth whispered before pressing kisses on his face as she sobbed.

Will tightened his arms around her. “There is no need to cry, my love. I live!”

“You do! I am so pleased it is all over!”

Her words ended the spell. “We must speak, dearest.”

“May I suggest my library?” Mr. Bennet said from down the hall.

“Of course, sir,” Will said.

Once in the room, Will explained the situation to his betrothed and her father. “I came here before approaching Wickham.”

“You do not think he has fled?” Bennet asked.

“No, we had men watching their camp.”

"Will this man testify against Wickham?" Elizabeth asked.

"I believe so," Will answered. "First, he will have to identify Wickham before the magistrate. I will leave now to see to it."

Mr. Bennet allowed the lovers a private farewell. When Will, at last, tore his lips from his beloved, he rode to Meryton, confident of his victory.

As he approached the house used as Colonel Forster's headquarters, Will's shoulders felt lighter than they had in years. The hired men had arrived with Bradley in tow. The magistrate had also preceded him. Bradley saw Will enter and begged for mercy.

"Just tell the truth, and you shall be rewarded," Will responded.

Colonel Forster was announced and scowled as he looked at Will. "Mr. Darcy, I understand you have a severe accusation against one of my officers."

"Yes, sir."

"The same that you visited me about before?"

"Just so."

Forster harrumphed. "Get on with it then."

Will told the story of his carriage accident and the apprehension of the man who fired the shot.

"And you swear that you were paid to cause this accident?" Forster asked Bradley.

"Yes, sir," Bradley answered.

"And you, Mr. Darcy," Forster nodded at Will, "acknowledge that Wickham could not have done this crime."

"I understand that he was on duty for the day. However, he must have arranged matters with this man."

"So, then all we need is to bring Wickham forward, and he should easily be identified."

Will nodded his agreement. Still, doubt tingled in the pit of his stomach. Could Wickham have had another man meet with Bradley?

Wickham was brought in and looked surprised to see so many people.

"Lieutenant Wickham," the magistrate began after introductions, "did you meet with this man and give payment for the intention of killing Mr. Darcy?"

"Certainly not, sir!" Wickham recoiled.

"Mr. Bradley, is this the gentleman with whom you met?"

Bradley frowned. "No, sir. You must believe me though—there was a man! I dunno Mr. Darcy and would have no cause to hurt him otherwise."

Wickham sighed in visible relief. Will had expected a smirk or a maniacal grin.

"Describe the man you did meet, then!" Will demanded.

"Mr. Darcy, I will ask the questions," the magistrate reprimanded. Will nodded his apology. "Could you describe the man you met?"

"He did not much look like this gentleman, sir. He seemed slight...elegant. It was strange as he was dressed roughly."

The magistrate and Will exchanged looks.

"Do you recall anything else?" the magistrate pressed.

"He had sandy blonde hair and his eyes...they seemed lifeless."

The magistrate jotted down some notes. "Where did this meeting take place?"

"The tavern."

Will whispered in the magistrate's ear. The man nodded and turned to Bradley once more.

"You described the man as elegant. What did you witness which struck you as elegant?"

Will observed the man. If it had been something obvious about his mannerisms, then others might have noted it as well.

"I cannot say," Bradley shrugged. "He was small, crafty looking. He thought well of himself, though."

"He carried himself with arrogance then?"

"Confidence or arrogance—I would not know. He wore as much authority as any master I have had."

"So, he did not seem to be a worker?"

"No," Bradley shook his head. "His hands were not rough."

"Can you remember anything else? Anything at all?"

"That's all, sir."

The magistrate frowned.

"You must believe me!" Bradley cried as the magistrate signaled for him to be carried away. "I have told the truth—I swear on the lives me children!" He continued to shout as he was carted off.

Forster looked at Will with raised brows. "It seems as though your business here is over, Mr. Darcy."

"Might I have a word alone with Mr. Wickham?" Will asked.

"Only this last time," Forster said, and the others left the room, leaving Will alone with his old enemy.

"Why?" Will asked.

"Why what?" Wickham returned.

"Why would you do this to me? Why do you hate me so much? What do you gain by my death?"

Wickham said nothing.

"You cannot think of marrying Georgiana. The parameters in my father's will are very clear. She cannot marry without the consent of Richard or me. She has many years before she comes of age. Do you think you can control her for so long? And when her brother has died with suspicion of it being at your hands? I do not care how you have manipulated her—she is too intelligent and loving to wish me dead."

Wickham only smiled.

"Say something!" Will demanded and beat his fists on the table.

The door flung open, and Forster came in. "That's enough bullying my soldier, Darcy."

Will grunted at the Colonel then threw a disgusted look at Wickham and left.

He left word with the magistrate that he would not press charges against Bradley before returning to Netherfield. The ride took far longer than usual. All the while, Will wondered how to explain this development to Elizabeth. Anxiety for her disappeared, however, when he was greeted with the tear-streaked face of Mrs. Annesley.

Full of restless energy after Will left, Elizabeth could not resist an invitation to walk to Meryton from Jane and Mary—even as they said Charlotte Lucas would be with them. Elizabeth had not made peace with her old friend yet. She was not entirely sure she could. It was forgivable that Charlotte had erred. She was very hurt by Sam and probably very embarrassed since Will had proved faithful. What Elizabeth wanted to know, however, was if Charlotte regretted her words. Did she think differently now? There could be no going forward if she did not.

“Will you not shake hands with me, Eliza?” Charlotte said, drawing close to Elizabeth. “I would wish we could be friends like we once were.”

Elizabeth sighed. “We cannot change the past. We cannot erase what has happened.”

“What of your philosophy to think only of the past as its remembrance gives you pleasure?”

“I do have many great memories with you, Charlotte. However, it is less certain if our friendship can continue.”

“Can you not forgive me?”

“Do you wish for it?”

Charlotte hung her head. “More than I can say. I greatly wronged you. Pray, forgive me, although I know I do not deserve it.”

Elizabeth smiled a little. “Forgiveness is never deserved, nor is it earned. I know you meant well. Can you wish me joy?”

“Indeed, I do!” Charlotte said with what seemed like genuine feeling. “Mr. Darcy seems a very worthy young man. I am happy to see that he is untouched by the behavior that afflicted S—” Charlotte gulped. “Your brother.”

“He is the very best of men,” Elizabeth sighed. She knew Charlotte only disliked Will because she had been so hurt by Sam. She did not even feel the need to ask her friend about her change in feelings. "I pray one day you may meet such a man!"

Charlotte shook her head. "Nay, such girlish dreams of true love are over for me. I delight in seeing my friends happy. And are we soon to wish Jane joy, as well?"

Elizabeth grinned. "Mr. Bingley has asked for an official courtship. I believe they are a fair way to being in love with one another. They met years ago when Will and I did, you know."

"I know," Charlotte nodded.

"Did you ever meet Will or Charles in the old days? Or Will's cousin, Richard?"

"No," Charlotte blushed. "The other day was my first meeting with Colonel Fitzwilliam. I know your brother enjoyed the company of all of them. I suppose it was only Sam that turned out so bad... and well, maybe Mr. Wickham."

Elizabeth started. "Whatever Sam's faults were they were nothing like Wickham's."

"No? Are you certain—" Charlotte paused when Elizabeth raised her chin, and her eyes flashed a warning. "I suppose you must know more than I do."

"Indeed." Elizabeth now extended her hand as Charlotte had done earlier. "Now, we may shake hands, my friend." The ladies smiled and clasped hands before quickly embracing.

"You all go into the shop," Elizabeth said as they reached the outskirts of the town and Jane and Mary had turned to discover her intentions. "I will walk up and down the promenade." She had hoped she could catch sight of Will as he left the encampment.

"You will be well on your own?" Jane asked.

"Of course," Elizabeth nodded. "There can be no danger in it," she said meaningfully to Jane, who subtly nodded her understanding.

Charlotte and Mary looked confused but did not question the other ladies. Elizabeth wished them happy shopping and walked along the streets of the town she had known all her life with more cheerfulness in her heart than she had felt in years. She was free to love! Their battles were now over, and soon she would be married to the man who had captured her heart so many years ago. She could hardly imagine a more blessed woman than she!

Her happiness bubbled up and shone through her face. She greeted acquaintances and strangers with a radiant smile few would ever forget. She had approached as near the encampment as she could go without risking her reputation. Intent on watching the road for some sign of Will, she was startled to hear a low voice from behind.

"Miss Elizabeth Bennet, you are as fetching as ever. The passing years have done you a great deal of good."

Immediately, Elizabeth trembled at the voice that had terrified her years ago. Whirling around, she came face to face with the dull, lifeless eyes and the predatory gaze of Lord Harcourt. Panic welled in her, but she caught herself before crying out.

"Ah, good girl," he smirked. "I always thought you were clever. You must understand that you would not wish to draw attention to us. After all, we are having a rather intimate conversation, and you are betrothed."

Elizabeth's eyes darted around. The situation did not look compromising, did it? Will would surely know she felt no pleasure with this conversation. Courage rising, she attempted nonchalance. "What brings you to Meryton?"

"The collection of a debt long owed to me."

His eyes raked down Elizabeth's body, and she shivered in disgust. "Who—" her voice cracked. "Who could owe you money here?"

"It is not just a debt that makes Meryton appealing."

"No?"

"As a dear friend of the bride's brother, I thought I would be allowed certain...liberties."

Elizabeth bit back her breakfast that threatened to re-emerge. "You were no friend to my brother."

"Why such vehemence? Are you not curious about the arrangement we came to before his death?"

Elizabeth gasped. Sam would never do what Harcourt intimated. "You lie!" She raised her hand to slap him, and he caught it.

"Do I?"

"Let me go," she spoke through clenched teeth as she attempted to pull free. Why had she wanted to walk so far away from the rest of the town?

"Your brother learned the consequences of not listening to my demands."

"You show your true character, at last, my lord," Elizabeth said. "I knew you would have some foul demand to make. I shall never capitulate."

She did not know Lord Harcourt well, but she doubted he would force himself on her on a public street. Indeed, he was too slight to pull her away.

His ego would not want that either. He would gain the greatest pleasure from her submitting to him. After she left his side, she would tell her father and Will, and they would provide protection while they searched him out. He was disgusting, but there was no reason to fear him.

"You are a feisty one," he said as he stepped closer. "I would be most willing if what you assume was the case. No, my request is only that you do not marry Mr. Darcy. You may keep your precious virtue—unless you would rather—"

"I will never offer that to you, and I will never agree to your demand."

"But of course," Harcourt laughed. "Why would you? After all, I have not explained why you should." He turned her to face the direction of the encampment. "You see, even now, your Will has learned that Mr. Wickham did not hire someone to spook his carriage horses. Indeed, the description his would-be assassin can give would match one given by townspeople of a certain village in Scotland. It would seem that George Wickham was not the man who killed your brother or Mr. Darcy's father."

Elizabeth's legs almost gave out as she understood Harcourt's meaning. She turned to look at her brother's murderer in the eye. She recalled the night at the theatre so many years ago. The noble before her had fooled everyone he met. Even now, he looked nothing like a madman. "You would kill him?"

Harcourt's eyes flashed, and his lips curled up, baring his teeth. "It would give me the greatest pleasure."

"Then why strike a bargain with me?"

Harcourt laughed and tapped Elizabeth's nose. "Yes, minx, you are uncommonly intelligent! I cannot hurt Mr. Darcy through his own death. It will only hurt others. However, separating him from his true love—well, that will wound him every day of his life. It is a pain that will only grow as the years go on—I should know."

"You were once in love?" Elizabeth tried to sound sympathetic. Perhaps if she could get him to speak more, she could find an alternative way to thwart his plans.

"No more," Harcourt shoved her away. "I will not tell you about my pain or more of my plan. Only know that I keep my promises. The choice is yours—protect the man you love or send him to his death."

Without another word, Lord Harcourt stalked off. Elizabeth could not chase after him, she could not call out. She did not want to create a spectacle, and it would be useless. A feminine crying spell would not work on his heart and change his intentions.

For weeks, Elizabeth had wondered at Will's feelings of responsibility and reticence to share his burdens with her. In the past few days, she had resented his single-minded determination to risk his life to rid himself of Wickham. Now, Elizabeth understood her beloved's choices. No tears came as her heart steeled with a decision. She could not—would not—marry Will.

Chapter Eleven

Elizabeth attempted to conceal her terror as she walked back to meet her sisters and friend. Fortunately, Charlotte needed to return to her home, and there was no need to hide from her perceptive glances. Once at Longbourn, Mary went directly to her pianoforte—in an effort to impress Miss Darcy with her improvement, she was becoming quite a slave to the instrument. Elizabeth knew she could not put Jane off for long, but pleaded a headache and hid in their chamber.

Once there, her head did begin to pound. She had not wavered in her intention. She must break the engagement to save Will from Harcourt—or at least delay it. Her lips turned up in a sly smile. The disgusting lord had not said that she could not share information with Will. The smile slipped from her face once she considered Will's reaction. He was not likely to take Harcourt's threat seriously. Nor would he consent to delay the wedding when only his life was at stake. Stupid man!

As Elizabeth wondered how she could possibly defer her wedding, a missive from Will arrived.

Guilt pricked at Elizabeth's conscience. Had she not been angry at Will when he had suggested the same? Her hand trembled as she opened his letter, feeling unworthy of the words of love she knew she would find.

Dearest Elizabeth,

I fear I do not have the joyful news we had anticipated. Bradley could not identify Wickham as the man who had paid him for his deed. The scoundrel himself refused to speak. I was unable to make him confess. I have failed you, my love.

However, it is only a temporary setback. Even now, I have agents searching the area for a man who matches the description given by Bradley.

I came home only to learn that Georgiana had left Netherfield after I had forbidden it. I recall our conversation on the matter and have told her this is the very last chance before she is sent away. Mrs. Annesley is now to be with her day and night.

I ask for additional forgiveness. It is selfish of me to ask, but I cannot conceive facing these trials without you. Years ago, I let you go when I needed you most. I will not make the mistake again. Will you, my dearest love, marry me just as we have planned? I have little but my heart to offer you and that you may not have long, but I vow no man will treasure any woman as I will treasure you.

All my love,

Will

Elizabeth could hardly breathe when she had finished. Will's love was all she had ever wanted in life. He offered her a choice with his request. She could ask for a longer engagement period. It would crush Will, though. He needed her at his side during all of this. She could not decide this on her own!

As though she felt her sister's distress, Jane knocked on the door and entered the chamber. "Mama wondered how you were," Jane said as she sat next to Elizabeth on the bed.

"I hardly know," Elizabeth said tonelessly as she handed Will's note to her sister.

Jane read and then turned her eyes on Elizabeth. "I am sorry that you do not have the answer about Wickham as we all had hoped. Is that all which makes you cry? Surely you will grant his request—

you have told me many times that you would marry him regardless of danger."

Jane's words felt like a knife to Elizabeth's heart. She exhaled sharply. "I would marry Will regardless of danger to myself."

"The danger to him is as it ever has been. What would cause you to reconsider now?"

Elizabeth remained silent as tears slid down her cheeks. She dared not even tell Jane about Harcourt's threat. Still, her words had been of use. "There is no time to explain it all just now," Elizabeth said as she turned to hug her sister. "Thank you for coming to me. All shall be revealed in time. Now, I must reply to his letter."

"Shall I ask the servant to continue to wait?"

"Thank you, no. You may tell him that Mr. Darcy will have his answer when he calls on the morrow."

Jane gave Elizabeth a curious look but nodded before leaving the room. Elizabeth remained in her chamber the rest of the day and hardly slept at all that night. When Will called the following morning, she refused to come down and would only entrust her letter to Jane.

As she heard the galloping of horse hooves a minute or two later, Elizabeth prayed he would read her words and forgive her. Even more than that, she prayed he could act the part.

Will forced one foot in front of the other as he walked from the stables to Netherfield. Elizabeth had refused to see him! The inexplicable pain from her first rejection, which he had thought healed, now emerged with more force than ever.

Without bringing Wickham to justice, he could never deserve Elizabeth. What man dared to ask a woman to marry him when he could only bring about her ruin? Wickham would either kill her or make her a widow. What could he do? Travel endlessly and never settle anywhere? Be subjected to Wickham's blackmail forever? Drain his coffers on bodyguards? Arrange for the unthinkable?

No! Will's conscience revolted. He would not stoop to what Wickham did. However, each possibility seemed more desperate than the last. Was this the course his life had been destined on since his father's death? Nay—even before. When was it that he had earned Wickham's hatred? What moment in time created the devil he now was?

Storming up the stairs and past the others in the drawing room, Will threw himself into a chair by the fire. He tossed Elizabeth's letter on a nearby table. It was all there if he chose to read it. All the ways in which he had failed her; all the reasons she had for breaking the engagement. He doubted not that he deserved every censorious remark. He had put her through more than any woman could endure.

Her smooth, feminine script bearing his name on the envelope mocked him. How many times had he wished to see a letter from her? Now, one of the few notes he had from her could not contain the words of love he had so come to cherish.

He glanced at the fire. Why should he keep this note which could only bring pain? He would watch it burn and shrivel just as his heart did.

A pounding on his door interrupted his plans. "Will! Let me in!" Charles yelled.

"It is unlocked," Will called back.

"What the devil are you doing in here?" Charles approached after opening the door. "You refused to greet your sister and Mrs. Annesley. I have never seen you so uncivil. What happened at Longbourn? We did not expect you back so early."

"I am afraid you will have to go on your calls alone from now on."

"What?"

"I will not be going back."

"What do you mean? You are speaking nonsense."

"It is all right there," Will pointed at the letter. "She has sent me away. She can no longer deal with the uncertainty regarding Wickham and the difficulties with Georgiana."

"She said that?" Charles inched closer. "Will! The letter is unopened."

"What else could she say? Yesterday all was well between us. Then, I reached another dead end with Wickham, and suddenly I am unwelcomed by her."

"Should you not at least read what she says? Did you forget how Elizabeth came up with an idea for subduing Wickham? Perhaps she has a new scheme."

Will paused. He wanted to tell Charles to bugger off, but the man had a point. "Very well," Will snatched the letter. "I shall read it."

Tearing open the letter, he willed his heart to withstand the pain.

Dearest Will,

When you read this, it is essential that you conceal your emotions if not alone. No one can know what I have written. Your very life may depend upon it.

Forgive me for turning you away so cruelly. My love for you has never waned and never will. I still desire to be your bride. I only ask that we delay it awhile.

Yesterday, Lord Harcourt approached me on the street. He confessed to being the man who set fire to the inn all those years ago. He promised to kill you if I did not break our engagement. He would say very little but said that he wished you to suffer more than even death could give.

Courage and honour does not exist only amongst men. I promised that I would, of course. While we plan otherwise, we must pretend that our plans are ruined. Once Harcourt feels victorious, he will surely leave for London. Then, we may marry in secret. He may then act rashly and expose himself or boast and give rise to witness testimony against him.

Can you act the heartbroken and rejected lover? Let no one know the truth. I want no chance of careless words to ruin this. Burn my letter when you are finished reading. Feel your heartbeat and know that every beat of my own lives for you alone. We need only be brave for a little while longer.

With all that I am,

Elizabeth

Will crumpled the paper in his fist before saying through his teeth, “Are you satisfied now?”

“Will—I—I apologise. I thought surely you must have misunderstood.”

“Do you wish to read it?” Will held up his hand.

“No—no.” Will tossed the paper into the fire and Charles hovered for another moment. “I will leave you.”

Once Charles left the chamber, Will sighed in relief. His lips moved an imperceptible inch. He applauded her plan but could think of one improvement. She had suggested delaying their wedding and then marrying in secret. Will rather liked the second half more than the first. They would marry in secret, only earlier than planned.

Will already had the license, and the marriage articles were now with his solicitor. He was sure he could arrange a private ceremony with Mr. Bennet. Perhaps Jane and Charles could be their witnesses.

Over the next few days, Will played the part of rejected suitor well. It did not take much effort. All he had to do was remember the days when he had thought Elizabeth did reject him. He must have performed well, for Charles frequently glanced at him with an anxious expression. Even Georgiana seemed to notice.

Two or three days after he had announced that Elizabeth called off the wedding, and pointedly explained it was because of Wickham but Georgiana's behaviour did not help, his sister came to him.

"Will," she said with downcast eyes. "Did Lizzy really cancel the wedding because of me?"

"I thought you had decided you were not close enough friends to call her so informally," Will said with raised brows.

Georgiana blushed. "I have spoken foolishly on many things." She squeezed her eyes shut and clasped her hands tightly in her lap. "Please, I must know. Have I ruined things for you?"

Will sighed. "I do not wish to hurt you." He placed one of his large hands over hers. "She is greatly put out with the difficulties we have faced. Knowing that even if Wickham is ever apprehended, she will have a sister who hates her and shows respect for no one added to her anxieties."

"I never thought my actions would lead to such." A tear slipped from an eye.

"Did you not? Was that not your goal?" He had not removed his hand, but his voice was not as gentle.

"It is what I said I wanted...what I thought would make me happy...but I had no hope I would succeed."

"You did not consider the consequences to your actions?"

Georgiana shook her head as the tears began to fall in earnest.

"Why did you behave so? Even before I returned to Hertfordshire to court Elizabeth, you were hateful to me. Ever since Ramsgate—"

"Do you not see?" Georgiana cried. "I was miserable and unhappy. I could only think of making others as miserable as me." Her lips trembled, and her breath came in shuddery gasps. "I suppose I managed that quite well."

"And do you feel better for it?"

"No!" Georgiana sobbed. "You have been such a good brother to me, and I do not deserve any of your kindness. Even now you are not scolding me or casting me away when I have destroyed your happiness."

"Did you bribe the express rider to never deliver Mrs. Annesley's letter?"

She nodded. "You have paid more attention to me in the last few months since I have been troublesome than you have in all my life."

Will watched as she buried her face in her hands. Her shoulders shook with the effort of her tears. At first, he was uncertain if she were genuine. Perhaps this was an added effort to gain information and pass it to Wickham. Will still believed Wickham was involved in some way.

"Have you been in contact with Wickham?"

Georgiana paled. "Yes," she whispered.

"For how long?"

"I never stopped corresponding with him after Ramsgate. I have not seen him here, though. I did not know he was here! He would sometimes reply to my notes but not for the last week."

"And it is this defection which has opened your eyes?"

Georgiana soberly nodded. "He used me just as you always said he did."

"Did you tell him anything about Elizabeth or me?"

"No. You told me nothing. Sure enough, he lost interest when he realised he could discover nothing through me."

"Why were you so miserable if he pretended to be the constant lover?"

Georgiana shrugged. "I knew nothing about our relationship was right. I knew I was hiding the truth from myself. I was so hurt and lost after Father died. And you...you were even more lost than me. I know now it was because of Elizabeth."

Will squeezed her hands. "But at the time, you thought I was rejecting you."

"You sent me to school."

"As was always Father's plan."

"But things had changed! Father had died—surely the plan needed to be reconsidered. Did you know I was afraid of inns for years?"

Will exhaled and squeezed his eyes shut.

"For years it would take days of travel from Pemberley to go to London. Night after night at an inn, and I had thought that if only you had let me stay at home..."

"I am sorry. I never knew."

"And there were times I refused to have a fire in my room at school. Did they ever tell you that?"

"No. How did you not freeze?"

"I would frequently wear every petticoat and pair of stockings I owned to bed." Georgiana chuckled at the memory. "The other girls found me peculiar, and I had no friends. Except for..."

"Except for when Wickham would visit you?"

Georgiana nodded, tears filling in her eyes once more. "I thought he was the only one who understood me."

"And now?"

"Now, I know he has only played the charming lover. I do not even know myself."

Will pulled his sister into an embrace. "We all lose our way sometimes. What matters is that we get back up, determined to right our wrongs, and do better."

Georgiana nodded against his shoulder. "I would acknowledge it was as you did with Elizabeth, but then I ruined that for you!"

"Do not fear for Elizabeth or me," Will patted his sister's back. "We do not know what the future holds. Years ago, I thought I had lost my only chance at her and happiness in life. Who says I will only have one second chance?"

Suddenly, Georgiana pulled back. Her face looked stony and determined, but her eyes held the old affection for her brother which he had not seen in months. “You must stop him, Brother. Do not rest until you do.”

A ghost of a smile appeared on Will’s face. “I thought you did not believe he was capable of hurting anyone?”

“I also thought I knew everything about him and everyone else. I am learning that I am not as wise as I thought. If you say there is proof of his misdeeds, I believe you.”

Happy at her words but conscious of what Elizabeth had cautioned about anyone knowing of their plans, he was careful with his words. “Wickham will be stopped at all costs.”

Georgiana smiled slightly and nodded. “I do hope you can forgive me. I was a selfish beast and never meant to cost you Elizabeth’s devotion.”

“You are my sister,” Will said. “I determined to forgive you long ago.”

The siblings embraced again before Georgiana left the chamber. Assured of his privacy, he wrote a missive to Mr. Bennet, stating his request. If Harcourt had a spy in one of the households or someone watching one of the houses, it should pass suspicion that Will needed to communicate with the man who was once to be his father-in-law. There were legal matters to resolve.

After sending the letter via Evans, Will sat back in his chair. Soon, he and Elizabeth would be married. Elizabeth's notion of drawing Harcourt out was as good as any. Will allowed himself to hope that someday, all their troubles would be at an end.

Chapter Twelve

Elizabeth had always hoped that Will would read her letter and agree to her plan. She supposed he would find a way to communicate with her. When she was called to her father's library a few days after she had refused to see Will, her heart skipped a beat. Sitting in her usual chair in the book-filled room, Elizabeth watched her father with anxious curiosity.

"Would you like to know what that Will of yours has suggested now?"

Elizabeth nodded. She had told only her father of her plans.

"He suggests you marry before Harcourt leaves the area."

"What?" Elizabeth had not thought he would reject her ideas entirely.

"In secret, of course," Mr. Bennet smirked as Elizabeth's affront eased.

"Would that be possible?"

"If it is first thing in the morning, and you arrive at separate times, then it might work. There are not generally people in the church or the surrounding area then."

Elizabeth sighed. "Mama will be unhappy. She had wanted a big wedding, and was just warming to the idea of my marrying Will at all."

"Indeed," Mr. Bennet said and thought for a moment. "Why not marry in secret now and continue to seem separated? Then, after Harcourt leaves, you might announce an intention to marry again. At this large wedding, he will come storming in to collect his price, and we will have guards in attendance."

Elizabeth slowly nodded. They would need witnesses. "Who can we trust to know?"

"Will suggests Charles and Jane."

Elizabeth frowned.

"You do not think they are trustworthy?"

"I worry that they will say something too transparent. We may be called upon to lie."

"You could keep it a secret and merely have Jane walk with you and surprise her once there."

"And after? She would not be able to contain her joy."

"I will go," Mr. Bennet said. "It would not appear unusual for me to have to speak with the rector. Surely, Will could trust his manservant."

"Very well. Does he suggest a day?"

Mr. Bennet chuckled. "Monday."

"Monday!" Elizabeth could hardly breathe. "Why, that is the day after!"

"You had best go," Mr. Bennet said as he pulled out writing supplies.

"Thank you." Elizabeth bent to kiss his cheek.

In her room, Elizabeth blushed to consider that at this time in two days she would be a married lady. She cast her eyes around the space. She had felt so grown up to join Jane in this chamber when she left the nursery behind. Now, it was fairly bursting, having to contain the accoutrements of two grown ladies. Soon, very soon, she hoped, she would be leaving it forever. She would not get to live as a typical bride and yet, just knowing she would be joined with Will in Holy Matrimony filled her with contentment.

She slept very little that night and even less on Sunday. On Monday, Elizabeth awoke at dawn and treated herself to a slow ramble in the morning mist. A few minutes before the appointed time, she approached Longbourn's church. None of the villagers seemed to be around. Most would be working in the house or at the estate. Mothers would be busy with their children. There was only old Mrs. Shaw that might be peeking out her window to see any comings and goings. Elizabeth looked in the direction of the small house the woman kept. She could see no one at the window. Even still, she affected a mournful countenance and posture. Any witnesses would think she approached the church for spiritual assistance. After all, she had broken an engagement and when the rumors of such circulated, many would consider her a fallen woman. They might as well carry her to the church themselves!

Inside, the pastor looked up from where he sat near the door to his office. He beckoned Elizabeth to approach.

“The others are in here,” he whispered. “My curate will wait here to lend assistance or diversion should we need it. Are you certain you wish for it this way, my child?”

“Yes,” Elizabeth nodded and smiled shyly.

“Then let us continue.”

Elizabeth followed him into the little room, and instantly her eyes focused on Will. They would be crowded anyway, but his presence seemed to take up most of the space. He smiled at her entrance and did not take his eyes off of her the entire time, even when introducing his valet.

Throughout the ceremony, Elizabeth's hands trembled. After all the wait, all the fear, she was marrying Will! She could scarcely believe it! In a matter of minutes, the legal ceremony was over.

"We will keep the register in here," the rector said. "Fortunately, it seems unlikely that we will have any other marriage applications for quite some time. Now, let us allow the Bride and Groom some privacy."

Mr. Bennet kissed Elizabeth on the cheek and joked that he would see her at home. Mr. Matthews said he would return to Netherfield.

Once alone, Will turned to Elizabeth. "I would kiss you, but I fear it too irreverent in such a place."

Elizabeth smiled and could agree with the sentiment entirely.

"I regret that this is not the ceremony you deserve."

"Think nothing of it. I surely regret more that I cannot live with you as a wife ought."

Will smiled so brightly it reached his eyes; fine lines formed around them. "How did you spend your morning?" He stroked her cheeks.

"I left early for a walk."

Will nodded. "I thought so. Your eyes are always brighter when you have been walking."

Elizabeth blushed and shook her head. "Where is the arrogant young man I knew? You do not think my eyes are brighter simply because you are around?"

Will suddenly started and frowned. He looked her up and down. "How long did you walk?"

"For several hours but the distance was not too far. I was too anxious to be far from the church. Why?"

"I thought to invite you to an establishment in Ware."

"In Ware!"

"It is not too far—scarcely more than the three miles you walked to Netherfield."

"What kind of establishment?" Elizabeth raised a brow. Her heart fluttered to consider what he would mean.

"Elizabeth," Will said in a low growl. "Can we not have some part of being husband and wife?"

Will's blue eyes stared intently at Elizabeth. The need in his eyes called on Elizabeth's heart. She shyly nodded her assent.

"The Rose and Crown. Do you know it?"

"Yes," she whispered. "W—when?"

"I will go very soon. My valet and carriage will soon leave for London."

"You are leaving?"

"No," Will hastened to interrupt her. "No, I will only look as though I am leaving. I will actually be in Ware. Harcourt should feel as though he won."

Elizabeth nodded. She should have considered that. What man would remain so near the woman who had rejected him?

"You will come?"

"I will. I suppose if I walk then I shall arrive around the same time you do."

"We should part," Will sighed and consulted his watch. "Soon, my love. Soon we will not have to separate."

Elizabeth nodded and watched as he left, her heart hammering in her chest as she considered the changes this day would bring. A few minutes later, the rector brought her to a less commonly used exit.

She walked first in the opposite direction of Ware, in case anyone had seen her at the church or was following her movements. Avoiding the main road, Elizabeth knew which paths would lead her to her destination. About an hour later, she stood outside of the Rose and Crown.

This was madness! What was she to do? Just go inside and...ask for a room? Ask for Mr. Darcy? Did he even register under his name? She had brought no things—but she was not staying the night, was she? So she was to go upstairs with a man and then return later and just walk out—without the proprietor thinking anything amiss? She was thankful Will chose a place so near Meryton. She did not have to worry about any friends or acquaintances needing an inn mere miles from their home.

Elizabeth turned and walked away. She would send a note later. Will would have to understand. She could not act in such a way. As she rounded the milliner, a figure emerged from the shop.

"Ah, there you are," a familiar voice said.

Elizabeth looked up in surprise.

"Should you be so astonished to see me, my love?" Will winked as a couple walked past them.

"I did not expect to find you at the milliner's," Elizabeth said with false sweetness.

"I must apologise. I realised after we parted that I had not considered how we might meet again and the difficulties you would have in finding me."

"Well?" Elizabeth raised her brows.

Will was silent for a long moment before he began chuckling. "Ah, I see my error. Let me amend my words. I do apologise. It was thoughtless of me. Can you forgive me?"

"I suppose I must. It must be part of my vows."

Cocking his head, Will smiled down on her. "I heard you promise to love, honour, and obey but not to forgive."

"Well, then you must command me to forgive you," Elizabeth said and flashed a saucy grin.

Will sucked in a quick breath before looking around. "Do you know, Mrs. Walker, I believe you now require rest."

"Oh, indeed, I must, Mr. Walker."

Will smirked but tucked Elizabeth's hand into his arm and nearly dragged her into the inn. Elizabeth contained a giggle at his eagerness. When he led her up the stairs, her legs began to tremble. Looking down at her, Will touched his forehead to hers just before opening the door.

Inside, Will drew her into his arms. Kissing her, he pulled on Elizabeth's bonnet ribbons. Elizabeth reached to assist him, but he swatted her hands away. He pulled back to whisper in her ear. "Tonight, I shall be your maid."

"I will stay?" Elizabeth looked around nervously. The room was furnished as most inns. She gulped at the large bed, then noticed some of her things. "What will be said of my absence from Longbourn?"

"Miss Lucas was prevailed upon to say you are staying with her."

Elizabeth frowned. "That story could not be held for long. If anyone asked her family..."

Will settled his hands around Elizabeth's waist. His thumbs rubbed in slow circles just above her hips. "Your father has convinced Sir William to keep his family quiet. He also knows of Lord Harcourt. The Lucases hate him almost as much as we do." Will paused and searched Elizabeth's eyes. "You are free to leave at any time—you are not my captive."

Elizabeth could not speak. Will had touched her more intimately before and yet she now felt drugged and incapable of resisting anything he would ask.

"Tell me what you are thinking," he urged. "It was a foolish plan; you resent my high handedness. Say something!"

"I think..." Elizabeth began, "you should kiss me again." Wrapping her arms around his neck, she pulled his head to hers.

Will awoke the following day to find his arms delightfully full of feminine softness. He nuzzled into the curve of Elizabeth's neck. "Good morning, Mrs. Darcy."

Elizabeth sighed happily and rolled over to kiss him. After many minutes in pleasurable distraction, she pulled back. "I suppose I should return now. When will I see you again?"

"Soon," Will said. "Perhaps three or four days. Whenever Richard can confirm that Harcourt is definitely in London."

"And then we shall have a ceremony before our family?" Elizabeth smiled.

"Yes, love. Richard's parents are eager to meet you again."

"Again?" Elizabeth's brow wrinkled. "Oh! At the theatre. I confess I had entirely forgotten they were there that evening."

Will chuckled. "How embarrassed my poor aunt

would be to hear her illustrious rank made no impression upon you."

"Forgive me for being too besotted and distracted to care for such lofty titles of personages that could mean nothing to me."

Will rewarded her words with a kiss. "Well, they have not forgotten you. The earl had originally planned to journey with us. They are very cognizant of what might have been and of what we lost that day."

"Did they know that you and I had an attachment?"

Will paused a moment. "I think they suspected it."

"Why?"

"I could not bear to hear Sam mentioned. Nor would I countenance any talk of a marriage for me—they thought I should consider marrying my cousin Anne more."

"Will they not approve of me?"

"No, that was never their complaint," Will shook his head. "They never wished me to marry without affection or would say you are too low. They were friends with your father, after all."

Elizabeth nodded.

"It is Lady Catherine who will rail at our marriage." Elizabeth tensed in Will's arms, and he held her tighter. "I do not care what she has to say. I never have."

"Did Anne wish to marry you?"

The question brought Will up short. He had never really considered it before. "I do not know."

"She is still unwed?"

"Yes," Will slowly said the word.

He searched his memory for interactions with Anne. Had she expected his addresses? Maybe. Had there been genuine hope or affection on her side? He doubted it. She neither sought him out nor acted embarrassed or flustered when he was near. Then again, he had never been particularly good at reading females.

"Never mind," Elizabeth snuggled closer. "It hardly matters. You did not raise her expectations and cannot be held accountable for every lady who hoped to gain your notice. I have won you, and I do not much enjoy thinking about other ladies and you marrying them in our marriage bed."

"Say it again," Will whispered in her ear as his hands ran over her body. A shiver racked her frame.

"That I have won you?"

He kissed just below her ear, drawing a moan from her lips. "Indeed, you have. Will you torture me, woman?"

"Hmm...perhaps, but I believe I have a new title now."

"Will you torture me, wife?" His lips wandered down her neck.

"I shall plague you every day, I am sure."

"Do you know, Mrs. Darcy, I think you sometimes talk too much." Will pulled Elizabeth's lips to his, where they were occupied until the sun reached high in the sky.

When they awoke again, Will whispered endearments in his wife's ear. She caressed his old scars and asked to hear how he had braved the fire attempting to rescue his loved ones. He held her close as he explained how she had healed his wounds. Although he did not fixate on hating inns the way Georgiana had, he carried the burdens of the fire with him for years. Now, he was beginning a new path and forging new memories.

At last, the time came that he must give up the comfort of his bride. In a hired hack, they rode first in the opposite direction of Meryton and changed routes several times before bringing Elizabeth back to the outskirts of Meryton. There, Miss Lucas would walk her back to Longbourn. It took some faith for Will to trust Miss Lucas, but Elizabeth had told him of her renewed friendship with Sam's former betrothed. Elizabeth's trunk had been directed to Lucas Lodge but Miss Lucas arranged for it to be delivered to the inn.

Will returned to his rented chamber at the inn, feeling more than ever that his heart resided outside of his chest. The only thing which eased the dull ache he felt at Elizabeth's absence was an express from Richard, explaining he had already seen Harcourt at his usual gaming tables. More than ever, he prayed Elizabeth's suggestion would prove right. He needed his wife in his arms once more.

Chapter Thirteen

Over the next few days, Will determined he had not been followed to the inn. Likewise, Elizabeth was able to pass along information via Charles. In the long days of loneliness and isolation at the Ware inn, Will wondered about Harcourt's intelligence. It seemed like he put too much faith in Elizabeth's vow to break the engagement. Then again, perhaps he knew that Jane and Charles were headed to the altar and Will and Elizabeth would always be in each other's orbit. It would add to Will's pain all the more if he would easily hear of Elizabeth but not have her for himself. Still, he did not appear to have other accomplices. Wickham must have only been designed as a distraction.

When Will read his name in a gossip column, he knew they had succeeded. Harcourt must have crowed to someone that Elizabeth jilted Will. If he had said that much, he might have said more. Will would wait a few more days before returning to Netherfield. Harcourt needed to feel secure in his victory. Correspondence from Mr. Walker of the Rose and Crown in Ware to Mr. Bennet of

Longbourn increased. A new wedding date was planned. The rector graciously agreed to their plans.

All in all, less than a week since becoming husband and wife, Will and Elizabeth were reunited. The night before the nuptials, the Bennet ladies dined at Netherfield. Will's London relations had arrived, but Elizabeth's aunt and uncle were to come in the evening. Mr. Bennet had gone to London to retrieve them. Will remained on unfriendly terms with Lady Catherine, and she was not invited to the wedding.

When the ladies separated after the meal, Richard laughingly queried Will about how it felt to be a married man. Although it was meant to be a secret, Will explained the situation to his uncle, Lord Fitzwilliam, and another cousin, a viscount named Francis.

"Harcourt has an awful reputation," Francis observed.

"People fear his ruthlessness," the earl countered. "Unfortunately, it gets him what he most wants: respect—or something very close to it." He shook his head. "I never would have guessed the son of a butcher could have such authority."

"He is the son of a butcher?" Will asked. "I thought his father was the last earl."

"He was," the earl nodded. "However, it was one of those unexpected and distant relative inheritances. The blasted war took all the closer relations."

"But a butcher?" Richard asked.

"Oh, the family had not fallen that much. His father had been a respectable clergyman, although he did marry a bit low. His wife was the niece of a rich butcher. Harcourt's father could have entered the church as well, but chose to take over his uncle's business. The war had inflated prices, and he could not resist the money."

Will furrowed his brow. There had been a certain roughness about Harcourt at Eton. He must have terrorized the other boys lest they do the same to him given his background.

"When his father unexpectedly inherited, it thrust the boy, Peter, into a new world," the earl continued. "I once thought he might have been a friend for you, Will."

"How so?"

"He inherited not long before you did. He was connected with the family—although, perhaps not as much as he would have liked."

"Pardon?" Will knew of nothing connecting him to Harcourt.

"The father knew the de Bourghs." Lord Fitzwilliam sipped his wine. "Sir Lewis' father had been a merchant in the same town as the Harcourt family. He was rewarded with a baronetcy at the end of the Seven Years' War. Blasted French." The men raised their glasses in agreement.

Will and Richard exchanged a look. "Father," Richard said, "tell us more about how the Harcourts knew the de Bourghs."

"Jacob Harcourt, your Lord Harcourt's father, and Sir Lewis were born in the same year. They grew up together in Ramsgate."

At the name of the seaside town, Will took more interest in the story.

"And you know Sir Lewis did not inherit until Anne was nearly ten." The earl shrugged. "Anne and Peter were playmates until she moved to Rosings and his father inherited the earldom."

"Was not there talk of a marriage between them?" Francis asked.

Lord Fitzwilliam nodded. "Yes, but by the time Peter inherited and was of age, Lady Catherine had fixated on Anne marrying Will. She did not approve of Peter's background."

"Fine talk, that," Francis grumbled. "Anne is only one generation more removed from trade, and surely an earl trumps a baronet."

"Not to mention the Harcourts must have been rich enough from the money they made on selling during the war," Richard added. "I am sure it was the de Bourgh money which appealed to Lady Catherine while she waited for her husband to inherit."

The earl furrowed his brow as though he searched his memory for something on the topic. Before he could say anything more, the clock chimed the top of the hour.

Will had heard enough. Harcourt might hate him because the man had not won Anne's hand, but why target Will's father? If killing Will was the real aim all those years before, then why wait so long to make a second attempt? It mattered not. Elizabeth was already Will's wife by law and the church, and on the morrow, all the world would know it. He was tired of waiting, and at that moment, tired of conversation with anyone other than his wife.

"We should join the ladies," Will said while standing.

The other gentlemen followed suit after some good-natured teasing on the subject of Will's lovestruck ways. In the drawing room, Georgiana, Elizabeth, and Mary took turns performing on the pianoforte. Will allowed their joined voices to wash over him. Soon, he hoped, Harcourt would make his move. He had once questioned his father about why he was on such friendly terms with Harcourt. Will now supposed it was not so strange if Harcourt was such close friends to the de Bourgh family.

As the Gardiners were expected at Longbourn by seven, the Bennets soon left Netherfield. Will pulled Elizabeth away for a private farewell. They would be recognised by all as man and wife after tomorrow. Charles had offered for them to stay at Netherfield, but Will was through sharing Elizabeth with others. They would travel to London after the wedding breakfast. Georgiana would stay with the earl and countess for a week or two. She had made many amends for her behaviour, but sometimes glanced anxiously at Will. He assumed she worried for his welfare or wished for his approval. He had made it clear to her upon his return to Netherfield that she was not permanently banished to their relations. Providing she continue to behave well, she could join them in a few weeks. He even offered the possibility of inviting Mary to town—an idea which all the ladies favoured and Bennet laughed at him for suggesting.

As he headed for his chamber for the evening, the earl pulled him aside. "I could not remember earlier, but Lady Catherine says that Harcourt recently tried to pay court to Anne again. She was too angry to admit defeat at losing you. She also objected to Harcourt's finances."

"Harcourt is known for winning at the tables and even acting as a moneylender. What happened to all the money?"

"I could not say," Lord Fitzwilliam answered. "Catherine was insulted by Harcourt's application."

Will thanked his uncle for the information and said goodnight. The pieces of information rolled in his brain as he attempted to sleep. His dreams bounced from Harcourt to Anne to Wickham to a smoke-filled Scottish inn. He awoke to a throbbing head, aching heart, and empty arms.

"Are you worried, Lizzy?" Jane asked as the sisters prepared for the ceremony.

"No," Elizabeth said more to herself than Jane. "Harcourt has already begun to behave as we predicted."

"What can be his motive? What about Wickham?"

Elizabeth sighed. "I do not know. However, Will and I refuse to continue hiding. It is time to begin our life together. If it is cut short, then I trust it was meant to be. We have already lost so much time..." Elizabeth trailed off as tears threatened to spill down her cheeks. She refused to give into painful memories or anxious fears. This was to be the happiest day of her life!

"I know one thing for certain," Jane said as she put the finishing touches on her sister's hair.

"What is that?"

"Will would never let any harm come to you."

Elizabeth nodded her agreement. It was a risk she was too selfish to take. She could not relinquish her right to Will and be done with the whole thing. If anything ever happened to him, she might spend the rest of her life wondering how life might have been different if only she had given into Harcourt's demands. She pushed the worries aside. If she did as he wanted, who knew if he would keep his agreement.

There was a knock on the door and Mary entered. "Lizzy, it's time," she said. "Oh! You look lovely!"

"Thank you," Elizabeth smiled at her sister.

"Will sent the carriage," Mary said. "It only seats six, so I will walk."

"Surely, that is not necessary," Jane said. "Papa can walk or take the horse. Or Lydia may sit on my lap."

Mary shook her head. "I would not want to wrinkle your gown and Papa should be there for Lizzy. It is no matter. I will leave directly."

"Very well," Elizabeth said before leaving her seat to embrace her sister. "We shall see you soon at Darcy House."

"I look forward to it!" Mary grinned. After a moment's hesitance, she left.

"Now, let us get you married," Jane said as she and Elizabeth walked downstairs arm in arm.

It was just as well that Mary walked to the church, for Mrs. Bennet made them load and unload the carriage several times before they at last left Longbourn. Elizabeth rolled her eyes at the entire thing. Many brides walked to the church—indeed, she had on the day they legally wed! Longbourn's church was less than a quarter of a mile away. Taking the carriage only made things take longer.

Entering the church, the family began to take their places. However, Elizabeth soon noted a disturbance at the front. Mrs. Bennet started shrilly crying for her husband and swooned into the arms of her sisters. After a moment of conversation, Mr. Gardiner and Will approached

Elizabeth and Mr. Bennet at the back of the church.

"What is wrong?" Bennet asked.

"It is Mary," Mr. Gardiner shook his head. "She has not arrived. We have already searched the path."

"Georgiana," Will's voice cracked, "is also missing."

"Could they be together?" Elizabeth asked, beginning to tremble.

Will nodded. "That is a possibility. She had desired to walk this morning, but I wanted to arrive early. Mrs. Annesley was to go with her, but when the others arrived, they informed me Mrs. Annesley awoke ill and was unable to accompany Georgiana."

"Mary never mentioned wishing to meet Georgiana, nor did she leave early enough, which would suggest her intention."

"She was very adamant about walking, though," Mr. Bennet reminded her.

"I have sent the guards, my valet, and Richard to search for them," Will said as he took Elizabeth's hands in his. "They probably merely lost track of time."

Elizabeth nodded even as uneasiness simmered in her. Behind them, they heard a slamming sound at the door. With widened eyes, Elizabeth watched as the three gentlemen rushed to the entrance. They could not get the door to budge. Outside of the church, Elizabeth heard shouts and women crying.

"Peter?" Elizabeth heard Mary's horrified voice. "Why are you doing this?"

Elizabeth ran to a window, hoping she could see the scene outside. She saw Mary fling herself at Lord Harcourt. He pushed her aside, and she landed on the ground with a thud.

"No!" Georgiana rushed to her friend's side. While there, she did not see Wickham approach from the forest. He quickly subdued her and had her bound by rope. Will had come to Elizabeth's side and watched with her.

"I must save her!" Will said.

"You do not know what they mean to do," Elizabeth said just before seeing Wickham pour what looked like lamp oil around the church. .

Will's eyes turned dark. He ran back to the door and shouted through it. "It is me you have a quarrel with, Harcourt. Let the others out!"

Elizabeth heard Harcourt's sickening laugh. "Oh, this is so much better than anything I could have planned. You will die with your love but know that your sister is now in my control. Tell me, how does Mrs. Wickham sound to you? I think your father might have enjoyed the idea of Wickham blood running Pemberley."

"I will never marry him! Never!" Georgiana screamed.

"Silence her!" Harcourt commanded. A smacking sound reverberated through the church.

In a cry of rage, Will charged at the door. By now, everyone was gathered at the front. Charles and the other gentlemen assisted Will, but it was useless. Elizabeth looked toward the windows. They were small, and it would take far too long to break through the lead cames—if someone could even slip through.

Lydia, Kitty, and Mrs. Bennet took equal turns wailing at their predicament. Elizabeth could no longer see anyone. Wickham had carried Mary and Georgiana away. Soon, smoke filled the air. Elizabeth tried to not despair as Will and the men continued to fatigue themselves as they beat upon the door.

Suddenly, a shot rang out. Then four more. Silence reigned—even Elizabeth's sisters and mother were too terrified to continue their tears. Soon, there were voices and shouting again. Elizabeth heard the splashing of water as the villagers who were nearby ran to put out the flames. At the door, there was a scratching sound accompanied by masculine groans. Finally, the door flung open, flooding the church with light and much needed fresh air. On the other side was a heaving Richard.

Will pushed past the crowd to come to Elizabeth's side. He led her outside, then released her arm to go back in and help the others.

Elizabeth saw the bodies of Wickham and Harcourt. Mary and Georgiana hugged each other under a tree. Mr. Bennet had gathered his wife and other daughters under another. Charles held a sobbing Jane. Elizabeth wondered if this was what battlefields felt like when the fighting ended. Casting a glance over her shoulder, she saw Will and his cousin assisting his aunt out of the church. His uncle helped the elderly rector.

Approaching Georgiana and Mary, Elizabeth wondered how they would ever know the reasons behind Harcourt's actions. She was only happy it was over.

"Mary," Elizabeth choked out. "I am so happy you are well! You too, Georgiana."

The girls held their arms open to her, and she fell into them. They were bruised but would survive. It could have been much worse.

"What happened?" Elizabeth asked her sisters through tears.

"I was to meet Georgiana and Peter for the wedding."

"Peter?"

"I believe Will called him Harcourt, but I only knew him as an errand boy named Peter who I had met in the bookshop. He charmed me when I first met him."

Sudden understanding filled Elizabeth. "You met him when we went shopping with Georgiana?"

Mary nodded. "It was our little secret. I felt so mature and worldly. I had a confidant in Georgie and an admirer in Peter." She crawled to her knees and pulled one of Elizabeth's hands in her own. "I am sorry for vexing you about Georgie and Will," she pleaded, "but you have to believe me I had no idea Peter was Lord Harcourt or intended to hurt anyone."

"You told him about the wedding?" Elizabeth asked.

Mary nodded as tears streaked down her face. "Yes. I had not seen him in days and was excited to introduce him to my family."

Elizabeth sighed. What had Mary been thinking? An errand boy? "Mary, surely you knew..."

"I liked his attention," Mary sighed. "You and Jane had your serious suitors. I only wanted a flirtation."

The sound of hoofbeats drew Elizabeth's notice. The magistrate, Colonel Forster, and the apothecary had arrived. Wickham and Harcourt were brought into a cottage. Elizabeth clutched her heart as she saw Harcourt begin to raise his head. He lived!

As if sensing her fear, Will approached. He led Elizabeth away from their sisters. "It is over now," he murmured as he held her close.

"He lives," Elizabeth forced out as sobs began to rack her body. She was no longer afraid, but her body released the tension in the only way it knew how.

"He will stand trial for attempted murder of many people—including an earl. He will hang if he survives. We are free."

Elizabeth nodded against his chest. They were finally free.

Eventually, the fright of the morning wore off, and as the sun continued to rise, Mrs. Bennet's nerves fluttered forward. It was nearly noon, and

Elizabeth and Mr. Darcy had not yet wed! When her husband explained that they were already legally married, she actually clapped in delight and called everyone to the wedding breakfast—even the villagers.

The breakfast was a subdued affair and not as light-hearted as Elizabeth had expected, but filled with even more joy than anticipated. In due time, Will and Elizabeth hugged their loved ones goodbye and departed for London.

During the ride, Will explained what he had learned about the events of the morning. The magistrate had managed to procure a confession from Harcourt before he died. He did not hate Will based on Lady Catherine's rejection alone. Anne had refused him, as well. She did not like his character as a gambler and a rake. She preferred an upstanding man like Will.

Harcourt had hoped to kill Will in the fire in Scotland. Wickham had only been his means of information about their location and useful in stealing Will's letters. He had not known of Harcourt's intentions, believing he just meant to extract his debt from Sam and harass Will. However, Harcourt soon blackmailed Wickham afterward, threatening to provide proof of his guilt in the arson. Believing Will suffered at the loss of Elizabeth, even if he had not died, provided a balm for Harcourt.

Before the Darcys left for Scotland, Harcourt approached George Darcy. He hoped to bribe the man to ensure his son would never marry Anne. Disgusted, Mr. Darcy had begun to expose Harcourt for the man he truly was, resulting in loss of status and income for Harcourt, who continued to live above his means, desperate to appear the wealthy nobleman and not the lowly butcher's son. As his income diminished, his contempt for Will increased.

While attempting to court Anne a second time, Harcourt learned that Will had arrived at Longbourn. His hatred rekindled, he posed as a hired hand in Meryton and had bought Wickham his commission in the militia. Wickham had continued courting Georgiana, but she proved unable to provide any information. Meeting Mary was merely chance, and yet allowed Harcourt the possibility of learning about Elizabeth. He had returned to Meryton to continue the flirtation.

"No more," Elizabeth silenced Will's lips. "I do not care to hear any more about Lord Harcourt or Mr. Wickham. In fact, I do not wish to think about them ever again."

"Shall we think only of the past as its remembrance brings us pleasure?" Will asked.

"Yes," Elizabeth smiled as Will kissed her lips. "And we will dream of the future while never taking a moment for granted."

"I like the sound of that, Mrs. Darcy," Will said.

"And I am happy to officially be Mrs. Darcy instead of Mrs. Walker! Whatever made you choose that name?"

"Do you remember, love? Miss Bingley described you as an excellent walker just before I saw you for the first time. I think I lost my heart to you at just that moment."

Elizabeth laughed. "It must have been, for the first thing I ever said to you was to reprimand. Oh, the conceit I had then!"

"As if I was any better," Will laughed.

"We are best together," Elizabeth observed.

"I am nothing without you, Elizabeth," Will said before drawing her into a kiss.

As it deepened, and more vows of love were murmured mixed with gentle teases and laughter, Elizabeth felt more treasured than ever before in her life. As she had promised, she thought of the future and, at last free of the past, she only grinned to consider what it held for them. Together, they would conquer anything.

Friends and Follies

Will and Elizabeth are safely married but what of their friends and family? Continue to enjoy Will and Elizabeth's marriage as their love touches the lives of all around them with a spin-off series, Friends and Follies. Read along as their family and friends' discover paths to their own happily ever afters. Continue reading for a teaser of Restored, Book One of Friends and Follies.

Sample of Restored

Coming 2019

Three Years Later

Elizabeth and Will stared at the markers in the ground. In between them with his tiny, chubby hands in one of their own stood their two-year-old son Bennet. Another child now grew in Elizabeth's belly. Jane and Bingley had married a few months after them and now had two girls. According to Mr. Bennet's will, the next Longbourn heir would be his first grandson who would not inherit an estate. Elizabeth placed her hand where the babe in her now kicked.

"We should name him after Sam," she said.

Will nodded. "I agree." He knelt to arrange the flowers she had brought. Upon standing, he lifted Bennet in one arm and wrapped the other around Elizabeth. "It is as we always planned."

"Not quite," Elizabeth sniffed.

Her eyes wandered to the patch of land next to her mother's grave. The physicians warned them Mr. Bennet would likely leave them before the year's end.

"I had thought they would be older," she said.

"True, but he is fortunate that his family may be near as his time comes."

Jane and Bingley had talked of giving up Netherfield and purchasing an estate closer to Pemberley, but at the news of Mr. Bennet's ailing health, they chose to stay.

"If it were many years from now," Will added, "your sisters might be married and living far away."

It mattered little that Pemberley was such a distance from Longbourn. Will took care of everything so they could be near the Bennets at this time. The thought always made Elizabeth's heart swell in love for him even more.

"We have been blessed," he murmured into her hair. "Bennet is healthy and strong. We have another little one on the way. We have had nothing to trouble or vex us since our wedding day."

Elizabeth nodded. When she considered that time in her life, she could scarcely remember any particulars. She only recalled the constant anxiety. For over two years, they had lived blissfully happy at Pemberley with visits to Hertfordshire and London.

The first Christmas was celebrated at their estate with everyone present. The next year, the Bingleys hosted. This year would be a subdued affair at Longbourn as Mr. Bennet could barely leave his bed.

London had been nothing for Elizabeth to worry about. They spent a few weeks enjoying the theatre and shops before retiring to Pemberley with Georgiana. When they returned in the Spring, the new Mrs. Bingley was making a splash. Who could dislike Mrs. Darcy when her sister was so angelic? Elizabeth knew, of course, they had not met with universal approval. However, they had experienced the ton without any extreme censure.

In time, even Lady Catherine had written to make amends with her nephew. At first, he was unwilling to accept any apology. However, Elizabeth advocated for peace in the family. He could not stomach visiting Rosings or seeing her face yet, but he replied civilly to her letters. For a time, Anne had visited them, and Elizabeth was happy to see for herself that the lady had no attachment to Will.

Mary continued to reside mostly with the Darcys. She and Georgiana were fast friends, spending the majority of the day at their pianofortes and clustered together in the evening. If they should dare to attend a ball with the Darcys, one never danced if the other was unattended. As such, both ladies were still unwed. They were only twenty, however, and had many years before they needed to worry about being on the shelf. On the whole, Elizabeth was pleased with how each lady brought out the best in the other. Although not sisters by birth, they were as close as Elizabeth and Jane.

Through the many seasons of the last three years, Will had provided Elizabeth with the support she always knew he would. She rejoiced to see his growth from friend and lover to devoted husband and father.

"Lizzy," Jane's voice interrupted Elizabeth's thoughts. "Charlotte is here and wishes to see Bennet."

"I will take him," Will said, and he kissed his wife on the cheek. "Do not stay out too long."

"Thank you," Elizabeth said. "I love you."

"Lub you," Bennet cooed.

"Aw, I love you too," Elizabeth laughed as she tickled the boy. His laughter lifted her spirits.

Before leaving, Will whispered in Elizabeth's ear. "These trials make us stronger, never forget that. I learned to love you during one, and it strengthened through another. Everything we now have we owe to them. I would not trade our love for anything."

"Nor would I," Elizabeth agreed. Will placed a soothing kiss on her forehead and departed with Bennet in tow.

Elizabeth sighed as she looked at the graves again. "I wish you were here, Sam. I think Papa would be more at ease if he knew the matter of the estate was settled before he went. There is so much I wish you could have known and seen. You would be the very best uncle to Bennet and Jane's girls! However, I have learned to accept what I cannot change. I have determined to find happiness no matter what life tosses me. Soon, you will have Papa with you just as you are with our mother and sister. I know he has missed you every day. Take care of him for us."

Elizabeth turned to leave, a feeling of peace settling in her heart. It was as Will had said. These trials would make her stronger. They had been very fortunate, and unfortunately, the demise of one's parents was a natural occurrence. Like the tress who lost their leaves in the Autumn and bloomed again with new life in the Spring, Elizabeth would accept this change.

She was so calm at the idea that she nearly missed a rasping voice say her name.

“Lizzy,” she heard again.

Turning, Elizabeth found herself looking into the unmistakable eyes of her brother.

Continued in Friends and Follies: Restored. Coming late 2019!

Acknowledgments

To my author friends Leenie and Zoe that always were willing to hold my hand, nothing can take your place in my heart.

Thank you to the countless other people of the JAFF community who have inspired and encouraged me.

Last but not least, I could never have written, let alone published, without the love and support of my beloved husband and babies!

About the Author

Born in the wrong era, Rose Fairbanks has read nineteenth-century novels since childhood. Although she studied history, her transcript also contains every course in which she could discuss Jane Austen. Never having given up all-nighters for reading, Rose discovered her love for Historical Romance after reading Christi Caldwell's Heart of a Duke Series.

After a financial downturn and her husband's unemployment had threatened her ability to stay at home with their special needs child, Rose began writing the kinds of stories she had loved to read for so many years. Now, a best-selling author of Jane Austen-inspired stories, she also writes Regency Romance, Historical Fiction, Paranormal Romance, and Historical Fantasy.

Having completed a BA in history in 2008, she plans to finish her master's studies someday. When not reading or writing, Rose runs after her two young children, ignores housework, and profusely thanks her husband for doing all the dishes and laundry. She is a member of the Jane Austen Society of North America and Romance Writers of America.

You can connect with Rose on Instagram, Pinterest, and her blog: http://rosefairbanks.com

To join her email list for information about new releases and any other news, you can sign up here: http://eepurl.com/bmJHjn

Facebook fans! Join Rose's reading groups:

Rose's Reading Garden

Jane Austen Re-Imaginings Series

Christmas with Jane

When Love Blooms Series

Pride and Prejudice and Bluestockings Series

Loving Elizabeth Series

Also by Rose Fairbanks

Jane Austen Re-Imaginings Series

(Stand Alone Series)

Letters from the Heart

Undone Business

No Cause to Repine

Love Lasts Longest

Mr. Darcy's Kindness

Mr. Darcy's Compassion (Coming 2019)

When Love Blooms Series

Sufficient Encouragement

Renewed Hope

Extraordinary Devotion

Loving Elizabeth Series

Pledged

Reunited

Treasured

Pride and Prejudice and Bluestockings

Mr. Darcy's Bluestocking Bride

Lady Darcy's Bluestocking Club (Coming 2019)

Impertinent Daughters Series

The Gentleman's Impertinent Daughter

Mr. Darcy's Impertinent Daughter (Coming 2019)

Desire and Obligation Series

A Sense of Obligation

Domestic Felicity (Coming 2019)

Christmas with Jane

Once Upon a December

Mr. Darcy's Miracle at Longbourn

How Darcy Saved Christmas

Men of Austen

The Secrets of Pemberley

The Secrets of Donwell Abbey (Emma Variation, Coming 2019)

Regency Romance

Flowers of Scotland (Marriage Maker Series)

The Maid of Inverness

Paranormal Regency Fairy Tale

Cinderella's Phantom Prince and Beauty's Mirror (with Jenni James)

Made in the USA
Columbia, SC
11 December 2018